LAKE *of* TEARS

Published by
TYRUS BOOKS
an imprint of F+W Media, Inc.
10151 Carver Road, Suite 200
Blue Ash, OH 45242. U.S.A.
www.tyrusbooks.com

Hardcover ISBN 10: 1-4405-7150-3
Hardcover ISBN 13: 978-1-4405-7150-3
Paperback ISBN 10: 1-4405-7151-1
Paperback ISBN 13: 978-1-4405-7151-0
eISBN 10: 1-4405-7152-X
eISBN 13: 978-1-4405-7152-7

Printed in the United States of America.

10 9 8 7 6 5 4 3 2 1

Library of Congress Cataloging-in-Publication Data

Logue, Mary.
Lake of tears / Mary Logue.
    pages cm
    ISBN 978-1-4405-7151-0 (pbk.) -- ISBN 1-4405-7151-1 (pbk.) -- ISBN 978-
1-4405-7150-3 (hardcover) -- ISBN 1-4405-7150-3 (hardcover) -- ISBN 978-1-4405-
7152-7 -- (eISBN)-- ISBN 1-4405-7152-X -- (eISBN)
    1. Watkins, Claire (Fictitious character)--Fiction. 2. Women detectives--Wisconsin
--Fiction. 3. Young women--Crimes against--Fiction. 4. Murder--Investigation--Fiction.
5. Wisconsin--Fiction. I. Title.
    PS3562.O456.L35 2014
    813'.54--dc23
                        2013031037

Cover image © 123rf.com.

This book is available at quantity discounts for bulk purchases.
For information, please call 1-800-289-0963.

LAKE *of* TEARS

A Claire Watkins Mystery

MARY LOGUE

TYRUS
BOOKS

F+W Media, Inc.

"War is a big and sprawling word that brings a lot of human suffering into the conversation, but combat is a different matter.
. . . There is a profound and mysterious gratification to the reciprocal agreement to protect another person with your life, and combat is virtually the only situation in which that happens regularly."

Sebastian Junger, *War*

AFGHANISTAN, KONAR PROVINCE

He was so tired he could hardly walk when *zing*, a shot screamed by. Sounding like the zip of a mega-mosquito, or maybe like a rusty door hinge moving fast, or like that inhalation of breath when you hit your toe and don't want to scream.

Back at the outpost, they'd always talk about what a bullet sounded like when it came close. It was like a contest, trying to name the sound.

First he was falling out, then he was on fire. The whole valley exploded. They were caught on a ridgeline, a hell of a place to be. An ambush, major contact. Sounded like the enemy was all around.

He started running; he'd never known how fast he could move with sixty pounds of gear. Another zip and he went to a low crawl. Then he was pinned down by gunfire. Caught. His buddies were there, then gone, sliding down the side of the mountain, ammo from an M2 tearing them up.

When he got hit, he knew it but couldn't believe it. Like he got punched in the head. From nowhere. Nasty.

All he could do was watch the other guys getting blasted. Falling.

One over the cliff, hanging on.

The world darkened. He was counting on the promise to never leave anyone behind, to never let go.

Promised with blood and swearing.

Then he saw those hands falling away.

He saw it all, then he, too, was gone.

CHAPTER 1

The tattooed flames on the man's shoulder were illuminated by the fire. He was standing right in front of Meg. She wanted to touch it. In truth, she wanted to put her lips to it. The roundness, hardness of the flesh that held the flames drew her. Had she turned into a moth?

She was standing just to the side of the man, packed in the crowd. Everyone had pushed toward the beach as the longship was set on fire by the torches that had been carried triumphantly through the crowd as the sun set.

The tattooed man stood about a head taller than her. He wasn't thin, but he wasn't fat. His muscles pushed at his skin, shouting energy. She had caught glimpses of his face, but couldn't tell how old he was. Maybe a few years older than her, but not too many. She guessed mid-twenties.

Meg hadn't thought she'd come down to the beach for Burning Boat, this weird, kind of new-agey thing some artists did annually down on the shore of Lake Pepin, which was actually part of the Mississippi. Her mom was all jazzed about it, but it had sounded kinda pseudo-cool to her. Like what old folks thought was far out. Build a Norse longship out of recycled pallets, and then burn it. Come on, a Norse longship? Where did that come from?

But Meg had nothing else to do. All her friends had gone off to college. Curt had left two months ago. Because Madison was so expensive, Meg had decided to postpone going to college until winter so she could earn more money at the Harbor View—the best and most lucrative season at the restaurant was fall, when the leaves turned.

After her mom and Rich went to the park, Meg had reluctantly followed them, walked down to the beach, figuring she could just go home if it was too boring.

But there was something about the ship on the shore that had grabbed her. It had been built on a small peninsula that stuck into the bay of Fort St. Antoine. As the sun set, the ship stood out in silhouette. Brave and alone, it awaited its fate, the dragon head facing the lake.

She had moved in closer, joined the throng that gathered on the sand close to the shore. Even though it was late September, the night was warm and still. People were wearing little. As the fire was lit, she noticed the shoulder of the man in front of her. The blue and red flames etched into his skin drew her eyes.

He shifted his weight and bumped her hip. He turned toward her, squinted his eyes, and said, "Sorry."

"S'all right," she said, and couldn't help smiling. He looked like a farm boy, with broad cheeks, ruddy skin, sun-kissed short blond hair. And so healthy. Like he drank a gallon of milk a day, and ran ten miles, and harvested wheat in his sleep. But a smart farm boy, who knew his way around a barnyard and knew how to coax animals to do what he wanted.

"Cool, huh?" He nodded his head toward the fire.

"Absolutely," she said, and it was.

"It's going to go fast," he said.

"How'd you know?"

"I know fire."

And Meg believed him. He was that kind of man. He didn't brag, but he let you know what he could do.

"That why you have it on your shoulder?" She reached out and did what she had longed to do—she touched a finger to his flames.

He jerked. Then he was embarrassed and moved back toward her. "I just had it done. Still tender."

"So it's brand new?"

"Yeah, last week."

"What inspired you?"

"To remind me of something. You know. Couldn't do it before, it was against regulations."

"What regulations?"

"Army. Got out a few months ago."

That's why she hadn't seen him around. "How long were you in the army?"

"Four years."

"Wow. That's a long time."

"You're telling me."

The longship was all afire, fore to aft. An amazing sight, as if a dragon had licked its tongue the length of the vessel. Meg watched it, but she was even more aware of the man standing next to her, only inches away.

"Where did you go?" she asked.

"Where?"

"In the army."

"I was in it deep. Afghanistan."

"Really?" While Meg knew about the war, knew that they had been fighting there for years, she hadn't really given it much thought. "What was it like?"

He had been smiling. He had been looking down at her with an amused look. But now he turned away, saying, "Too long to tell."

She felt like she had made a mistake. They had been talking so comfortably, and then she had asked the wrong question. Maybe it was private. Maybe he didn't want to talk about it. She had touched his tattoo, and it had hurt. She had asked a question, and that had hurt, too. Time to move to comfortable ground.

"Nice fire," she said.

"Not bad," he said, and gave her a quick glance.

The sound of crackling filled the air. The sky grew darker, and the ship sparked high in its light and flames. The orange and white flickering against the dark, the brightest yellow.

Meg could feel his body heat next to hers. "I'm Meg."

The tattooed man, the army man, turned to her and leaned over, his face close to hers, his smile a hint, and said, "I'm Stickler. Andrew Stickler."

Andrew, she thought. Not a bad name. Kind of old-fashioned, but that was okay. Her name was, too.

"You live around here?" he asked.

Meg took this as a good sign. She was glad he asked. She didn't have a boyfriend anymore. After almost three years, Curt and she had decided to release each other from their going-steadiness, as much as it had hurt. This decision had seemed very grown up at the time, two months ago. But she had been feeling very lonely since he had left, and looked forward to his frequent e-mails. Now she was glad that she was free.

"Yup. Just outside of town."

"I live by Durand. For the time being."

Not far away. Still in the county. "Oh, yeah."

The ship began to sink into the fire. The dragon's head tilted, then fell. The crowd sighed and moaned with the conflagration. Meg felt small jolts inside her body. Andrew was standing closer than he needed to be, closer than the crowd demanded. He was a hair's breadth away from her. She had touched him.

"Can I get your number?" he asked.

"Sure. You got something to write it down with?"

He pulled a pen out of his jean pocket, but had no paper. He offered his hand to her, and she wrote her cell phone number on his palm.

"Don't take a bath," she said.

"Not before I call you," he said.

The ship collapsed. Something inside her was falling, too. She wanted to get away. She couldn't stand being so close to him but not touching him. She didn't know why. This had never happened to her before. Like she was in lust, in rut, whatever you wanted to call it. Maybe it was the heat of the day, the fire, but whatever it was—she wanted him.

"Okay, then," she said. "I'm going to head out."

"Be careful," he said. He reached out and tugged on a lock of her hair. "Don't get lost in the dark."

❧

"I love this ritual—offering a bonfire to the gods—but it reminds me we're losing the light." Claire leaned her chin on Rich's shoulder. He rubbed the top of her head as they watched the fire burn down to embers.

"The autumnal equinox. Yup, the nights are winning."

"But it was a nice summer. Nice and uneventful," Claire sighed. The worst crime that had been committed since April was a kid who had gone on a crime spree and stolen three computers from the high school. They'd caught him the next day when he tried to sell them on Craigslist. She called that a pretty good season.

"Don't jinx it."

"Maybe we should try to get away for a long weekend. Go up north now that the leafers are gone. Meg can take care of the pheasants."

"Claire, she can't take them to market."

"Just a couple of days?"

"If we went before next weekend I could squeeze it in."

"I'll find us a cozy cabin and we can snuggle for a few days. Leave the daughter alone."

"She seems a little lost without Curt."

"I know. It's sad. I was afraid that she would follow him to his college in Vermont when he couldn't get in to Madison. I'm proud of her decision to go forward with her own plans."

"Oh, she takes after her mother—too self-sufficient."

Claire thought of Meg, how she had seemed to bloom in the last year or so, growing her wavy brown hair into a long braid down her back, wearing clothes that suited her lanky body, even putting on a dab of lipstick once in a while. Her awkwardness was fading as she grew up. Too bad she couldn't find a new boyfriend for the next few months, someone to gang around with, to show her that there were more men in the world than Curt. Although Curt had been perfect for her in high school and might be perfect again, Claire wanted her daughter to know more men, to choose a man to be with because he was the best, not because he was the only.

As she watched the fire settle down to embers, she couldn't help but think what a nice burial it would be: wrapped in a cloth, laid in the bottom of a vessel, and set out onto the water in a shroud of flames.

❧

As Sheriff Talbert drove away from the Burning Boat spectacle, he felt like something was stuck in his throat. Maybe he had inhaled too much smoke. But for a few weeks now he hadn't been feeling that good—out of breath, nauseated, achy. He figured it was something that was going around. He had to watch that he didn't complain too much to Ella, or she would get on him to go to the doctor.

He hated doctors. They poked him like he was a bloated cow and told him he should lose half the weight he was carrying. Fat chance. Not with the way Ella fed him—pie and cookies and bars. She had been raised to cook for the field hands and, even though he wasn't a farmer, she fed him as if he were one.

He wondered if any of those coconut-chocolate pecan bars were left. His mouth watered just thinking about them.

Ella had ragged on him not to go tonight. "Why do you always feel like you have to be there? The deputies can handle it without you."

He didn't dare tell her how much he still enjoyed standing in the middle of the road, telling the cars where to go and talking to everyone, his community in the best of moods, joking and laughing and having a good time. He wouldn't miss it for anything.

No moon tonight and it was dark as the bottom of a well, driving up the coulees toward the top of the bluff. He had the windows open, as it was just the right temperature to put your hand out the window and let it drift on the breeze.

Just as he was turning at Pleasant Corners, he felt something stab him in the chest—a ripping feeling, as if an implement had been thrust into his insides and turned.

He let go of the wheel and slapped his hands on his sternum to make the tearing stop, but the pain got worse and rose up into his mouth like a wave of bile. The car didn't make the turn and plowed into a cornfield, the stalks ticking on the underside of the carriage and scraping the doors.

The car came to a stop deep in the corn.

He could hardly breathe, and the ripping pain made him feel faint. He tried to get out of the car, to get to the road, but he couldn't move his arms. He couldn't even turn off the car. The lights shone through the corn and he felt like he was looking at soldiers marching toward him, the lines going on and on.

CHAPTER 2

The sound of the birds chirping outside her window woke Emily Jorgenson. The first thought that flew into her mind was, *I hope my pot's okay.* She couldn't wait to see how it had turned out. Just so long as it hadn't broken. Mrs. Adams, her fourth-grade teacher, had warned them all that the pots might break in the heat or get smashed by the wood of the boat collapsing on top of them.

She slipped off her nightgown and scrambled into her jeans and T-shirt. The sun was up already. She had to go to church later, but she could run down to the park before then and find her pot.

After eating a bowl of cereal at her mom's insistence, she was finally allowed to go down to the beach. "Be careful of that fire, Emmie. Use a stick to stir around in it. It might still be hot."

She promised to be careful and skipped part of the way down the hill, then ran until she reached the highway. Since she had turned ten, Mom let her go anyplace in town she wanted to. But she had to promise to look both ways at the highway. "Those cars and those darn motorcycles come whipping through town too fast for their own good," her mom said.

A couple of motor homes were in the park, but she didn't see anyone outside. She loved having the park to herself, and was glad when summer was really over and all the campers went away.

Then she could run around without feeling like she was disturbing anyone. Her mom said that the campers made money for the town and that was good, but Emily still wished they wouldn't take over the park every summer, especially during the very nicest days.

Emily could see the dark burned spot on the small island where the longship had been. Technically, the spit of land wasn't an island but a peninsula, because it was sort of attached to the shore. She had learned that in geography.

She wouldn't waste any time this morning looking for arrowheads or agates, two of her favorite things to do. Once she had found a lovely pink piece of stone that had been worked all along one edge, and her dad told her that it was a part of a spear, because it was so large. Emily put it in her treasure box. But one of her biggest wishes was to find a real, complete arrowhead.

She walked down the beach until she reached the path that went out onto the peninsula. A faint fishy smell wafted over her. She didn't mind it. The lake smell was a mixture of all sorts of stinks—weeds, water, and even a sun scent.

As Emily walked up to the burned spot, she held her breath—both because it was still smoky and because she was nervous about what she would find. She remembered exactly where she had put her pot—right under the dragon head on the longship—so she would be able to find it easily. She watched her step, walking just beside the scorched grass where rubble and charred bits of wood were strewn on the ground. There sure wasn't much left of the ship.

She pulled a willow branch off the ground and ripped the leaves off. It would be good for poking around in the ashes.

Her pot was a small round bowl made out of tan clay, about the size of her fist. She jabbed at the area where she thought she had placed it. After using the willow branch like a rake, she uncovered what at first looked like a clod of dirt. She stepped nearer, watching where she put her feet. Squatting down, she looked at the dark object more closely.

Emily could tell it was her bowl by the edging. She had pinched the edge just like her mom made pie crust. The pot had turned almost black, with a crack snaking down one side, but it was still whole. She gingerly touched it, but it wasn't too hot. After hooking the willow branch into the middle of it to scoop it up, she carried it to the water and rinsed it off. Some of the darkness washed off but much of it stayed on the pot, making it look like the pattern on a cowhide. Her teacher had called this kind of pot making *raku,* and said it was a Japanese word.

She wondered how the other kids' pots had turned out. Holding her bowl carefully, she walked back to the burned spot. As she stood to one side and the sun shone on the ashes, she saw a weird pattern of white sticks in the charred remains of the fire.

Emily put her pot down in the sand, took her willow wand, and poked at the white sticks. As she rubbed away the flakes, her stomach turned.

A finger was pointing at the lake. The white sticks were bones. Something clicked in her mind and Emily knew she was looking at a whole skeleton, stretched out in the ash.

‹›

"They're taking me to Mayo," Sheriff Talbert told Claire as she sat close to his bed. He had a private room in the hospital in Durand, which was right up the hill from the county offices. He was whispering and seemed to have aged ten years since she'd last seen him two days ago. "Quadruple bypass surgery." He held up a hand with four fingers pointing skyward.

"Can't do stents?" Claire asked.

"Too far gone. They need the big guns for me." He gave a throaty chuckle that turned into a cough.

"How long will you be out?"

"They can't say. I pushed 'em, but they want me to do therapy and all that crap. I hate to think what this will cost." His big meaty hand fell on Claire's and he grabbed her hand tight. "But I want you to be in charge of the department. I'm appointing you sheriff in my absence."

Sheriff. She had thought she might like that title in front of her name someday, and she wasn't getting any younger. She could retire in four years if she wanted to, and she had even considered it. "What about Stewy?"

"He don't want to be sheriff. Hell, he just wants to retire next year and buy a motor home. That's all he talks about these days. I can't ask him to take this on."

"Well, I don't mind stepping in for you, but it won't be for long, will it?"

"Who knows. Maybe they'll tell me I need less stress in my life. Ella has been saying that to me for years."

Ella had stepped out for some coffee a few minutes after Claire had arrived. Claire was pretty sure she just wanted to give them time to talk alone. She probably knew what her husband was going to ask Claire.

"She wants to go to the Grand Canyon. She's always wanted to, but somehow it didn't happen when the kids were young, and then the job got in the way, and I don't know where the time went." He rubbed his stubbly face. "I think it's time we went to the Grand Canyon. I'm kinda afraid of heights, but she hasn't asked that much of me over the years. I figure I can do this for her."

"Sounds like a good idea."

"So you can be in charge?" he asked her.

"Until you get back on your feet." Claire wanted to reach out and pat his leg, but he was not a touchy kind of guy. "Just so long as you don't fall into the canyon."

"Who knows how this is going to turn out," he said, patting his chest gently.

"It will turn out fine. You're going to the best place. They really know what they're doing at the Mayo."

"Yeah, but they're going to have to cut open my chest. I've never been cut open before. Gives me the willies."

"You'll be better than ever."

"I guess." His voice dropped.

Ella stepped back into the room. "I think that's enough talking for now. He's got to rest up for his trip. They're taking him by ambulance this afternoon."

"You'll keep us posted?" Claire asked.

"I've talked to Shirley at the department three times today already. She'll come and find me if I don't call."

"When's the surgery?" Claire asked.

"Next week. Sooner the better, I say. Get it over with."

The sheriff had fallen asleep. Claire and Ella looked down at him. Ella's face was tight. "I just want him to be okay."

❧

Amy hated to leave her bed on Sunday morning, one of the few times John didn't have to get up before her. His lips barely moved when she kissed him goodbye, then he rolled over and started to snore. It was everything she could do not to climb back in bed with him.

She started her shift at eight A.M. and rolled through Durand, checking things out, then circled back to the department for another cup of bad coffee. The big news this morning had been about the sheriff. She still couldn't believe it. Shirley said it was lucky he was alive. If his lights wouldn't have still been on, who knows when they would have found his car, buried deep in the corn.

Two teenagers had seen the lights and called it in. At the moment the car was sitting out front in the parking lot. Looked fine. But she heard the sheriff wasn't doing so good. She wondered briefly who would be in charge while the sheriff recovered. One thing she knew for sure was it wouldn't be her.

Shirley hollered back to her. "Got something you better check out in Fort St. Antoine. Some kid found some bones."

Bones, that sounded good. Something to do. It had been awful quiet lately. School had started; less time for kids to get in trouble.

"Where in Fort?" Amy walked up to the front desk.

"Down in the park. Claims they were in that burn they had there last night."

"You mean that big ship they set on fire?"

"I guess so."

Nice morning for a drive up the river. Few people on the road. Those who she passed were probably heading to church, and drove slowly and thoughtfully. The backwaters of the Chippewa and the Mississippi looked like the dark steel of an old knife in the early light.

Fort St. Antoine was one of the smallest towns in the county, but one of the busiest. Located in the far northern section, it was the closest to the Twin Cities and pulled a lot of tourists down with its interesting shops and arty activities. The Burning Boat celebration was the latest idea. Build a big boat, then burn it down. Lots of people didn't think it was such a good idea, but Amy thought it was kinda cool. She would have gone last night, but she had gone to dinner at John's mother's house. Since she and

John had moved in together, they'd made it a point to get out to see her at least once a week.

When Amy reached the park, she saw there were still two motor homes tucked under the cottonwood trees—the last of the season's campers. A pickup truck was parked on the shore near to the leftovers of the burn. Amy pulled the squad car in next to it and got out.

A tall, angular man and a small round girl were standing near the burned spot on the piece of land that stuck out into the river. As Amy walked up the man helloed her, and the girl stood a little closer to him.

"Jake Jorgenson," he said and held out his hand. They shook. He then put his hand on the little girl's head. "My daughter, Emily."

Amy held out her hand to the girl. Emily hesitantly reached out her hand, which felt like a soft animal in Amy's palm. Amy gave it a gentle shake. Emily's face broke open in a smile. The young girl was missing one of her bottom teeth.

"What did you find here?" Amy asked.

"Some bones." Emily twisted her mouth, then said, "But I didn't touch anything."

Mr. Jorgenson nodded toward the charred remnants of the boat.

At first all Amy could see was the burned rubble of the fire, but as she walked closer and studied it more, she began to make out what looked like the shadow of a body, lying on its side. From there she was able to visually pick out the pieces of bones, even though they had been discolored by the fire.

"Emily found this when she came looking for her pot," Jorgenson explained.

"We stayed here to keep other people away," Emily piped up. "So nothing was disturbed."

"That was good. You're a big help," Amy said. She looked up at the Jorgensons again. "Any chance this was part of the deal? Part of the Burning Boat show?"

"Not that I know of, but you'd have to talk to the organizers. I just came down when Emmie told us what she'd found, after I called the sheriff."

Amy walked in a little closer. The structure looked like human bones, a small person or a large child. She hated to think about who it might be. Hopefully no one she knew.

"I didn't touch anything," the young girl repeated, stepping out from behind her father's legs. "I just came to get my pot."

"So what's this about a pot?"

"Mrs. Adams, that's my teacher, she helped us to make pots and then we put them in the bottom of the boat. Well, really on the ground, kinda under the boat. That way when the boat was set on fire the pots would get baked and be real hard."

"When did you do that?"

The young girl looked up at her father. He nodded and said, "Go ahead, Emily. Tell her what you know."

She continued, "I think it was about three o'clock on Friday. I'm pretty sure, because we did it right after school and school gets over at ten to three. The guy who was the boss of the fire said we could do it when they were all finished with the boat. He showed us where to put the pots so they would be in the fire." She pulled a dark round object from her pocket and held it out in both hands. "This is mine and it didn't break or nothing. It's supposed to look like that, dirty and all. That's what Mrs. Adams said, and it's called raku."

"Very nice. So your whole class came down with your teacher and put the pots in the boat on Friday?"

"Everyone except for Ricky Jordan. He had to go home and help with the chores. Dinky Baker put Ricky's pot under the boat though."

"You didn't see anything unusual when you did that?"

"You mean like a body or anything?"

Amy stifled a burp of a laugh. "Yes, I guess that's what I mean."

"No, just a lot of willow branches. They were, like, all woven together. It made like a fence, and the boss guy said they would burn good."

"Okay, so you were here between three and four on Friday."

Emily squinched up her face and stared at Amy. "Does that give you a clue?"

"It does."

"Is this like a mystery?" Emily asked.

"So far, it is. But maybe there's a logical explanation."

"I know what that means. Logical means, like, understanding it. That it makes sense."

"Something like that."

"Otherwise this might be somebody who's dead and you would have to find out who did it."

"That's a possibility."

"That's enough, Emily." Her father wrapped an arm around her shoulders. "We need to get back home and get ready for church."

Amy squatted down so that her eyes were at the same height as Emily's. "You've been a big help. I'll take it from here, but I might be talking to you again."

Emily's face flashed a smile and she looked up at her father. "Sometimes I talk too much, but sometimes that can be good, right?"

"Yes, often it can be good."

CHAPTER 3

The lull of the summer was over. Claire knew that before she even saw the burned bones. She knew that their respite was done when she saw the way Amy was standing to the side of the large burned spot on the small spit of land that stuck out into Lake Pepin. Amy shifted her weight back and forth, her shoulders lifted up. She had already started carrying the crime.

Claire took her time getting out of the squad car. No hurry. The bones weren't going anyplace. At least this scene wouldn't be bloody. That was a blessing. She walked down to the beach, jumped over the small stream of water that separated the peninsula from the mainland, and stood next to Amy.

Amy pointed.

Claire followed her hand down, and at first just saw burned ends of sticks and grass scorched around the periphery of the fire. Then her eyes adjusted and the sticks turned into bones, turned into a body curled into the darkness of the burned-out fire. From what she could make out, the body had been lying on its side, arms pulled in to its chest, legs tucked up to its body. The posture looked like the fetal position, except for the hands, which weren't turned toward the chest, but stuck out defensively.

Fighting. It almost looked like the person had been fighting the fire.

"I suppose this could have been an accident. Someone drank too much and crawled in here to sleep. But it doesn't seem like it," Amy said. "Oops, I accidently fell into a burning boat."

Claire felt like laughing. There was nothing funny about what they were looking at, but she often found laughter built up inside of her like some awful gas when she was faced with a heinous crime. Laughter trying to push away what she was seeing, what she might have to face—someone put another person into the bottom of the boat, hoping they would burn away to nothing at all.

How could this have happened? How could one human being do this to another? And worse yet, it was probably someone she knew, passed in the grocery store, filled her car with gas next to them. Sometimes she hated the world, just hated knowing how bad it could be.

She exhaled slowly out her nose, then filled her chest with new air. "Nope. Hope it was an accident, but I've got a bad feeling."

"I called Petey. He's grabbing the camera and he's on his way."

"Good. I want lots of shots, and not just of the bones and the fire, but of the whole area."

"Got it."

Claire continued, "I don't want anyone to touch anything. Nothing. Don't move a twig until we get the forensics done on this. Let's cordon off all the way to the road. Keep people away from the beach, too. Don't let any campers come in and pitch their tents or park their three-wheelers. Although I'm not sure it's worth the effort; after all, there were about five hundred people down here last night. Who knows what we'll be able to find."

Amy glanced up at the sky. "I hate to tell you this, but it's looking like it might rain."

Claire stared west, across the river, the direction their weather came from. A slow slurry of iron-gray clouds was moving in. At least the clouds didn't look like they would produce a thunderstorm, but they still needed to act fast. "Shit. We need to put up tarps. Take care of that. I want the whole area not just cordoned off, but covered."

Amy craned her head up toward the sky and then asked, as if the clouds might know the answer, "What do you think? Do you think someone did this? Put the body in the boat?"

"Could be. I've seen it before. Some guy murders someone and then tries to burn the evidence, thinking they can completely burn a body—which is pretty hard to do—and that if there is no body, they can't be charged with a murder, which is not true either. In Minneapolis, some guy killed his wife, then put her body in the car and started it on fire. When they managed to put the fire out, he told the fireman that she had been drinking and smoking and probably set herself on fire. The medical examiner noticed the bone fractures in her skull when he was doing the postmortem. Traces of her blood were found in the kitchen on the rolling pin, of all things. Some argument gone very wrong."

Amy smiled at her. "Thus ends the lesson for this day."

"Okay, but you asked. Get on the horn and get some tarps down here. We need to get this area secured."

"Yes, ma'am."

Claire looked at the ground around the burn site: trampled grass, weeds bent over, but surprisingly, not much of the surrounding area was burned. She had seen the fire department at the scene last night, the guys leaning against their red behemoth, enjoying the spectacle. Maybe they suggested to the crew of the Burning Boat project to wet down the grass around the boat before they lit it on fire. Wouldn't be hard to carry water up from the lake.

She walked up to the remnants of the fire and squatted down, getting her first real close look at the bones. They were not that easy to see, discolored as they were by the fire. If you looked for them, they almost disappeared. Like one of those Magic Eye games where if you squinted your eyes or blurred your vision, you could see the outline of the bones more easily that way.

Claire leaned in and smelled the damp smokiness of the burn. The skull looked like one of the malformed pots the kids had made, turned on its side, its eye sockets like holes in a bowling ball. It looked like a couple of the ribs were broken, and she wondered if this had happened as the boat had burned, wood collapsing on top of the body—or if it had happened before the body had been moved to the boat.

A bundle of bones, that's all that was left of someone who was probably alive a couple days ago. Claire had the urge to touch the delicate finger bones of the hand, but resisted. *Do not disturb them.* Before this was over, she would have her fill of these bones.

After the photos today, they would need to get a forensic crew down to sift through all the ashes. Maybe they'd luck out and find a ring or some other piece of jewelry that would help identify the body. These days, not many people walked around without jewelry on. She looked at her own hands. Her wedding ring, which, even though it was bad luck, was a river pearl. That's what she had asked for. And she wore a simple pair of gold hoop earrings.

Just as Claire was pushing herself up, surprised at how creaky she felt today, she heard a shout as Amy yelled at someone to stop. A forty-something man wearing a baseball cap and jeans was trying to climb over the crime scene tape.

Amy grabbed him by the arm and he put his hands up. "Sorry, sorry. Just wanted to know what's going on here."

Claire recognized him as Stewart Richards, one of the artists who was in charge of Burning Boat. "It's okay, Amy. We need to talk to him."

"What's going on?" he asked. "Someone lose something?"

"How late where you here on Friday night?"

"The night before the burn? We quit on the early side. For once everything was ready on schedule. Doesn't happen very often. I'd say we left the site at about eight-thirty." Stewart screwed on his hat more tightly. "Why? What's happened?"

"I'm sorry to say we have found the bones of a body in the boat. Any ideas of how it got there?"

He swore into his hands. "Sorry. For real? What do you mean, a body? An animal?"

His surprise seemed genuine. Claire looked him in the eyes and said, "A human body."

"Geez. And they burned?"

"Incinerated." Claire decided she might as well ask the next question. "Anyone missing from your crew? Anyone not show up who worked on this project?"

"I don't think anyone's missing. I have to confess that I wasn't in the best shape yesterday at the burn. Pretty exhausted. Pretty torqued from the burn. Hard to keep track of everybody. There were students who came from the college I teach at, to work on the piece. I'd have to check around. My wife, Ellen, might have a better idea. She's back at the house."

"Why don't you give her a call and ask her to come down here? What are you doing here now?" Claire asked.

"Just checking to make sure the fire was out and to see what kind of mess we had to clean up." He shook his head. "You know, this is horrible, but we joked about the funeral pyre we were building. I can't believe it came true."

∽

When Doug woke up, he found himself in his car with his head leaning forward on the steering wheel. Watch showed ten hundred hours. Aching. Cold. Stiff. But safe and in his own car in the United States of America. He had to remind himself of this blessed fact. No enemies. No crazy mofos jumping out of the bushes.

He wasn't really sure where he was, but he knew he was not far from his grandma's house in Winona. That was where he was aimed. Didn't have any other place to go. His folks had thrown him out a couple weeks ago. After he lost his job, after he freaked out on them one too many times.

He pushed back the car seat, felt in his pocket for a cigarette. When he lit it, he let the match burn down until it was a moment away from his fingers. Just for practice. How close can you get without dropping it, without letting it get you. He'd spent hours in the OP doing that, staring at the flame before it burned him. Trying to not think about what was all around him. Not to think about the biggest monster he had ever known, a monster with a million legs, like a grubby old centipede, climbing over the mountains and coming after them. It spit fire, that monster, it chewed up rocks, nothing stopped it.

He needed to clean up a little before he went to his grandmother's. Stop and get something to eat, although probably the first thing she'd want to do was feed him. He remembered she was a good cook. He hadn't seen her in over four years, before he went overseas. He wondered how old she would look. He wondered what she would think of his new face.

He wouldn't stay there long.
Just long enough to deal with Andrew.

෴

"Could you get us a list of everyone who worked on this project?" Amy asked, looking at Ellen Becker-Richards, who was married to Stewart Richards and the codirector of the Burning Boat project.

Ellen was in her early forties, Amy would have guessed, but looked younger and dressed very young. She was wearing workout shorts and a ripped T-shirt over a long-sleeved shirt. Her black hair was pulled back in a ponytail and tucked under a matching baseball cap—which read, not surprisingly, Got a Match? Amy was avoiding saying Ellen's full name because she hated saying hyphenated names—they just bugged her. Why couldn't they either keep their own name or take their guy's—why make the whole world suffer from their indecision?

"I think I could put a list together. I'm not sure we have one. People kinda come and go."

"Your husband mentioned that you had some help from students of his. Were most of the people from outside Pepin County, or did you also have people helping from around here?"

"I'd say it was about half and half. All told, we probably had about twenty to twenty-five people working on the boat."

"Is anyone missing? Did any of the students not show up?"

"Not that I'm aware of."

"If this body was put in the boat on Friday night, why would no one have seen it on Saturday?"

"I'm guessing because the boat was pretty much done. Any work we did to it on Saturday was really external—piling up brush, clearing around it. But we were working on the lanterns on the beach and the other art pieces in the park."

Amy wrote down a note.

"I have a question for you." Ellen folded her arms over her chest. "Why do you think that whoever did this has a connection with the project?"

"We don't know, but it's a place to start. How would anyone even think to do this if they didn't know about the boat?"

"Yes, but everyone knew about the boat. The whole community has been watching us build this for the last few weeks. It's no secret."

"You're right. But like I said—it's a place to start. Actually, it wouldn't surprise me if they had a connection. Otherwise what would they be doing around it? Either to hide in the boat, or put someone there."

Ellen unfolded her arms and dropped them down to her waist, then tilted her head back. "This is not exactly the kind of publicity we had envisioned coming of this project."

"No, I don't imagine."

"But unfortunately, it fits with one of the uses of a longboat."

Amy wasn't sure why she had said that. "What do you mean?"

Ellen looked at her funny. "Aren't you Scandinavian?"

Amy shook her head. "Matter of fact, I'm not. Scotch-Irish. Why?"

"Well, longboats were often used to bury the Viking leaders. They'd lay them out in the bottom of the boat, light it on fire, and push them out to sea."

"Never knew that."

"Someone knew what they were for. That's probably what made them think to use it that way." Ellen looked around at the tarps going up. "Boy, you're really gearing up here."

"Gotta protect the evidence."
"You think you'll figure out what happened?"
"We usually do."

CHAPTER 4

The rain swept in with some wind as evening fell, enough to cause the branches of the cottonwoods to waltz along the shoreline. Claire was sitting in the squad car parked right outside the crime scene barriers, waiting for the bone guy to show up, a forensic osteologist. An official member of BARFAA, of all things. What a name. Stood for Bioarcheology and Forensic Anthropology Association—either they had a great sense of humor, or hadn't figured out what the acronym would spell out.

The bone expert was coming all the way from Madison, so he might not show up for another hour or so. Dr. Herman Pinkers. What a weird name, she thought. But then, what a weird profession, staring at bones all day long, trying to get them to tell you a story. Maybe not so different from what she did—examining shards of a leftover life, trying to figure out how and why it ended.

An old Volvo station wagon pulled up and a very tall, very thin man with silver-framed glasses perched on his nose got out. He was wearing khaki pants, a black turtleneck, and a vest with a million pockets. On his head was a broad-brimmed canvas hat.

She opened her car door and got out, saying, "Dr. Pinkers?"

"Hello. I'm here about the bones," he said.

"I'm Deputy . . . " she started to say, and then realized that wasn't who she was any more. "I'm Sheriff Watkins."

"Sheriff." He held out his hand.

She shook it. "Doctor."

"What've you got for me?"

"Follow me. We can get under the tarps, away from the rain." As they walked over to the burn site, she explained what had happened.

"They built a boat and burned it?" he asked.

"Yes, it's like the Burning Man thing. I guess kind of an ancient fall tradition. Like Guy Fawkes."

"Or Halloween," he suggested. "Fire to fight off the falling light."

"Yes, exactly." She brought him to the edge of the burn. "We've touched nothing. I wanted you to be able to see it as it was found, and also, I'd like you to be the one to extract the bone pieces. I just wasn't sure that anyone else should do it."

"You've photographed all this?" he asked.

"Yes, very thoroughly, early today, in good light."

"I can't work tonight, not in this rain," he said.

"No, I thought you might not be able to. I've got someone on duty here all night. I don't think it's supposed to rain tomorrow."

"I'll start as soon as the sun is up."

"That's about seven-fifteen."

"You are a farm girl," he commented dryly.

"Have to be around here."

"Let me just have a look." Pinkers folded his body so that he was close to the ground, then he reached up to his hat and turned on a light fastened to the underside of the brim. It was like a mining light, and it shone wherever he was looking. Sounds came out of him as he hovered above the bones for a few minutes, talking to himself, humming, almost grunting.

Claire stepped back and let him work. She knew how much she hated someone looking over her shoulder. She was tired and hungry and worried. The sheriff was going in for surgery bright and early tomorrow morning. She almost felt like praying for him, if she believed in that sort of thing. The rain shrouded the lake, the sky, as if pulling curtains from the bluffs.

Dr. Pinkers came and stood next to her, looking out over the lake. "Well, I'm guessing it was a woman. A young woman, but past puberty."

"How can you tell?"

"As I said, it's a guess, but the size of the pubic bone in the pelvis. A small woman who wouldn't have put up much of a fight."

☙

Not exactly the way Andrew had hoped to spend his Sunday night, sitting alone in the dark in a squad car, guarding the bones of a burned body. He could see the two of them—the doctor and Watkins—standing out in the rain, facing the lake. While he was used to taking orders, he wasn't used to not being in on the decision-making process. One more adjustment he had to make to civilian life.

When he had joined the Marines, he had been working in law enforcement for only a year, so coming back he had nil seniority. He would never catch up with everyone who had started in the sheriff's department at the same time as he had. After all, he had been gone for over four years, off and on. His last deployment to Afghanistan had been for nine months, a long tour of duty.

Now the two of them were walking back to their cars. After saying something to the tall man, Watkins headed toward his squad car. Andrew rolled down the window. She leaned in.

"You going to be okay to stay the night?" she asked.

What a question. Did he really have a choice? So like a woman to ask that. "Yeah, fine."

"You've had dinner?"

"I grabbed a burger before I came."

"There're johns over there." She waved toward the back of the park.

"I know."

"Someone will relieve you around eight in the morning."

"Do you really expect anyone to come around here tonight?"

"Not really. This is just a precaution, to establish chain of evidence. More to keep the scene safe from curiosity seekers. With this rain, I don't guess we'd get many of them. Also, look after those tarps. If you see any problems, make sure they're tied down. I'm going to take the doctor to get a room in Pepin."

"So he's the bone expert."

"Yeah. Seems to know what he's doing. Got enough coffee?"

"To swamp a horse."

She thumped the top of his car and turned to leave.

"Hey, congrats on being our new sheriff."

She turned back. "Thanks. Not exactly the way I wanted to get that title. We'll see what happens with Sheriff Talbert. I'm hoping this assignment is just temporary."

As Claire Watkins walked away, Andrew hoped it wasn't. He thought Sheriff Talbert was at the end of his run. Everything Andrew had seen about Claire told him that she could more than do the job. She was clear and quiet under pressure. She knew what she wanted and asked for it. Not that she didn't have emotions— sometimes they played out on her face, but not in her voice, not in her manners, not in her orders.

She would have made a good army officer.

He shut his eyes for a moment. Everything in his life was still overlaid with the war, with the fighting in Afghanistan. As if he was seeing through a film. This rain reminded him of the storms that would brew over the mountains, then come crashing down on top of them in the night, like the worst artillery barrage.

Back four months, and he was still living over there.

The life he had left was not what he had come back to—no apartment waiting for him, girlfriend gone to another.

With darkness closing in around him, the wind blowing the cottonwoods overhead, Andrew felt like he was sitting in a tank again, waiting for the enemy to show. That was always the hardest time, right before the fighting started, waiting for the world to explode in ways you couldn't even imagine.

He held out his hand and it was shaking. It was going to be a long night. He leaned his head back against the seat and took the long deep breaths the therapist had taught him. All the way from the belly, all through the body. Calm down.

Having bad nerves was no fun, but what was worst was that he wasn't the same. He had lost something he didn't even know how to describe. The film he was looking through made everything seem dull and lifeless. Nothing much excited him. He had to force himself to do things with old friends, even to get up in the morning. He felt like he had run a very long race and he just couldn't get his wind back. But even that didn't quite describe what he was going through.

What he really felt like was that he had been gutted.

☙

His voice sounded older than she had imagined, deep, smooth, and somehow in charge. He didn't say his name. He just said, "Hey, how's it going?" and she knew who it was.

Meg was so glad she had been the one to answer the phone. Somehow she didn't want her parents to know about this guy yet. Mom wasn't back from work, and Rich was in the other room, checking out something on the computer. Since they had gotten Wi-Fi in the house, he spent a lot of time online, even more than she did.

"Hey," she said back. "It's going good." She had waited hard all this day, wondering if he would really call. It was a good sign that he had called so soon after they met, even if it was rather late, certainly too late to do anything.

"What're you doing?" he asked.

"Not much. Hanging. Doing boring stuff. My laundry."

"Good for you. Might as well be productive."

"What're you doing?"

"Oh, I'm on the job."

"But you can talk?"

"Yeah, nothing much else to do. Just watching it rain."

"Yeah, I know the farmers need this rain, but it's kind of a drag."

"I shouldn't talk too long. But I was just wondering if you felt like getting together sometime this week."

She would have agreed to going for a ride that night, but he was at work. That was probably good—didn't want to appear too anxious. She hadn't dated anyone except Curt, so she didn't really know how to do it. "That'd be good. I could manage that. When were you thinking?"

"You, with your busy schedule?" he teased.

"Yeah, it actually is a busy schedule. I work a couple nights this week."

"Where do you work?"

"At the Harbor View."

"Pretty swanky."

"I guess. It's good money. Nice people."

"I've eaten there a few times. Food's not bad. Kinda rich."

"But I don't work tomorrow night," she couldn't stop herself from saying.

"You're off tomorrow night? Same with me. You want me to come and get you, we can go do something."

"I work tomorrow afternoon, but I get off at three. You want to pick me up after that? At the Harbor View? It's closer to Durand."

"You remembered where I lived. Sure, that sounds good. What do you want to do? Any ideas?"

Meg thought that all she really wanted to do was be in a dark car with him close. What was the matter with her? Where was the girl who wanted to get to know someone before there was any physical contact? "I don't know. You want to go for a hike? We could go up to the Maiden Rock."

"The Maiden Rock? I thought that was private property?"

"You've been gone for a while, haven't you. It was given to the Land Trust a couple years ago. They put in a nice hiking trail."

"Sounds good to me. Then we can get something to eat. Probably some place other than the Harbor View."

"Yeah, probably that would be a good idea," she hiccup-laughed, surprised how nervous she felt.

There was an awkward silence. "Okay then. See you at three at the Harbor View, Meg."

"See you, Andrew." She listened to him hang up the phone. She would see him tomorrow. She was glad he was going to pick her up at the Harbor View. Meg knew she could go out with whoever she wanted to—after all, in another few months, she would be out of the house, totally on her own. But she still wondered what her parents would think of her going out with someone so much older.

Her mom and Rich had told her that she didn't have a curfew anymore. She could stay out as late as she wanted to. Funny, now that she had permission, she had no one to stay out late with.

But maybe tomorrow night.

CHAPTER 5

"She's been gone since Friday," the man's voice came over the phone in a cross between a snarl and a shout. "That's three whole days."

"And who am I speaking with?" Amy asked, taking a sip of coffee. She didn't get nearly as riled up when people shouted at her as she used to when she first started the job. Everyone always thought that absolutely everything was an emergency. She had learned from Claire to take it slow and get the facts before she started to go bonkers.

Besides, she had only come on duty a couple of minutes ago, hadn't even finished her first cup of coffee. It was barely after eight in the morning and she had been looking forward to a quiet hour or two, straightening out her desk, filling out reports, catching up on things. Claire had gone to the crime scene with the bone expert, said she didn't need to be there until later.

"I'm her fiancé. We're getting married right before Thanksgiving. She said she'd give me a call last night. Never heard from her."

"Okay. But what's your name?"

"Terry. Terry Whitman."

Amy didn't recognize the name. "And where do you live?"

"Here in Durand. I moved here a couple years ago. Used to live in Woodbury, in Minnesota."

"And who's missing?"

"Tammy Lee Johansen."

The name buzzed through Amy's brain. She knew Tammy Lee. A couple years ahead of her in high school. Big blond girl with lots of teeth. Pretty, but not super bright. "Does she live with you?"

"No, not yet. We're trying to find a place, but she still lives on her own. We thought we'd wait until after the wedding. I think her folks would like that. But we see each other nearly every day."

"So the last time anyone saw her was on Friday?"

"Yeah, that's what it looks like. I thought she was at her folks', her folks thought she was with me. So no one missed her until late Saturday when I called over there. Her mom said she hadn't come home Friday night. We both figured maybe she had gone into the Cities to see her sister. She does that sometimes. Couldn't get in touch with her sister. So we weren't too worried. But then her mom talked to her sister last night, and Tammy wasn't there. We started checking around. Nobody has seen her since Friday. Her mom's not too worried, but I am."

Amy couldn't help but think of the bones they had found. But Tammy had probably gone to see a friend for a couple of days. She must be in her mid-twenties, with the big wedding event happening, and decided to take a break from life. Amy felt like that once in a while.

"Why don't you come in and fill out a missing person's report?" Amy suggested, as he seemed somewhat calmer.

"Okay. She could be hurt or kidnapped. I mean, what if something really bad has happened to her?"

"We will start checking into it. Have you called the hospital? Other friends? Does she work?"

"She isn't supposed to be at work until tonight. She works at the Pump and Dump. I haven't checked the hospital. Figured they'd call us if something bad happened. I've tried a few of her friends."

"Does she have her purse?"

"Yes. Her mom checked her place and it's not there, so she must have it."

"What about a car?"

"Her car is gone, too. It's an old Chevy, nothing special."

"Listen, come on in. We can't do anything until we have all the information. I'll be here all morning. We can go over the contacts you should try that will help you find her."

"Okay. Yeah, I'll be over."

Amy didn't know why she asked, but sometimes she didn't know when to leave things alone. "Did you two have a fight or anything recently?"

"What?" The snarl came back into his voice. He yelled, "You think this is my fault?"

"Just asking. I know a wedding can be a stressful time. Even a small quarrel can sometimes cause someone to take off for a few days."

"Tammy and me aren't like that. I wouldn't hurt her in a million years. We've never had a fight."

How unusual, Amy thought.

ॐ

Sitting in front of the TV, watching Oprah with his mom, Andrew knew he had to move out of his parents' house. He couldn't believe he was nearly thirty and back home again. But he was finding it so hard to do anything constructive, and the thought of all that was involved in moving out stymied him— finding a place, dealing with a landlord, new furniture, cooking. But maybe worst of all, being alone.

He hadn't had a minute to himself for years. In Afghanistan, he had bunked with a whole slew of guys, shoulder to shoulder sometimes. As bad as the situation had been over there, you were never alone.

When he was alone the bad feelings were the worst. They would swarm him. He felt like that girl Pandora who opened the box. If he didn't have something to take his mind off of what had happened, it all came rushing back at him, biting, insisting on taking over his mind.

At least at his parents' he could hear them moving around, his mom cooked great meals for him and was constantly talking, the TV was always going, Dad had his radio on downstairs, the dog was in and out of the house. The house was never quiet. He was reminded, all the time, that he wasn't over in Afghanistan anymore. No more war. He was finally home.

"I think she's gained a few pounds again," his mom said.

"Who's gained weight?" he asked.

"Oprah, she really struggles with it." His mom slapped her full stomach under a knitted sweater. "I know what that's like. But not you. You're still skinny. I thought after a few months of eating my food, you'd start to put some back on."

"I have, Mom. About ten pounds."

"Man, you were thin when you came home. Andrew, what did they feed you over there?"

"You don't want to know, believe me. Just packaged stuff that we could scarf down. Different colors, but tasted all the same. Good old MREs."

"What's that mean?"

He laughed. "The army never likes to say the full words to anything. Everything's always a code or an abbreviation. MRE stands for Meal Ready to Eat. A typical MRE would have some meat, a starch, peanut butter, always peanut butter, and then your candy. Oh, and moist towelettes. Can't forget those. Don't want to get your hands dirty." He could feel his anger rising in him, just talking about the food they ate. No wonder he didn't say much to his parents about what had gone on over there on his tour of duty.

Andrew stood up and walked to the back door. Being scared had made him hungry, and being hungry had made him scared. His mom wasn't the best cook in the world, but he was so happy to be eating her meatloaf again.

Still hours to go until he could pick Meg up. He hadn't had a woman in his arms in way too long. He'd have to watch himself so he didn't eat her up. She had seemed as fresh and sweet as a strawberry the other night. Andrew wondered what she was really like; he wondered if he would find out.

He sat down on the stoop and watched the farmer in the next field haying. His dad was talking about taking another pass through the fields. The weather was staying pretty good. Wasn't supposed to rain again until next weekend. That would give the hay enough time to dry in the field.

His shoulders slumped. Often he felt like he was still carrying something on his back. Hard to get over that feeling after always having gear hanging off of you. And he still had unfinished business he had to take care of.

The first thing he swore he would do when he got home was get in touch with Doug, and he hadn't even done it yet. Andrew had dialed the number for Doug's parents a couple of times, but then he'd hung up before the call went through.

Doug had been his best buddy over there. Doug, and Brian. They had been the reasons he had made it through. Without them, he would have lost it. He was sure of that. They made him laugh. Especially Doug. He could just be unbelievably funny, rude as all get-out. Infantile fart jokes, raunchy sex jokes, stupid knock-knock jokes. Whatever it took.

He had to know how Doug was doing, after what had happened, but he was afraid to find out. He wasn't even sure Doug would talk to him. He wasn't even sure Doug could talk.

When a guy got shipped out for medical reasons, they often got no news of them back at the outpost. It was like they just disappeared off the face of the earth.

That was the thing about Afghanistan that most people didn't get. It wasn't the United States. Being over there wasn't like real life. More like one of those weird horrible episodes of *The Twilight Zone* where nothing is the way it's supposed to be, and just when you think you've got it figured out and you wake up or you escape, then it gets even worse. Then you know you really might not make it out alive.

❧

"Can I do anything to help?" Claire asked as she watched Pinkers carefully step up to the site of the bones and then curve over the area, his back forming a perfect U-shape. In that moment, he so reminded her of an egret—even the slow and deliberate way he moved was like a bird picking his way through the shallows.

"Please stand back," he said without turning in her direction. "I can use your eyes, but I need to do this myself. I'm going to take a few quick photos of the site and then I'll start to remove the bones."

"We've taken extensive crime scene shots already."

He turned his head toward her without changing his position. "I understand, and I'm sure they're of higher quality than what I will take, but I need to have my own record. I know what I'm looking for. This will help me recall the position of all the bones so I can reassemble them in the lab."

"Right." She trusted him. His very weirdness made her trust him more. She could tell he was so focused on his work right now that he didn't even want to talk to her. Time to be quiet and just watch him.

She took a couple of steps back and surveyed the whole scene. A crisp fall morning by the lake. The thermometer had read just above freezing when she checked it at six. But the sky was clear and the sun was well above the bluff line. The day would warm up nicely, maybe even get into the sixties.

Claire had never worked with only bare bones before. Not only did she not know who the murder victim was—and murder was what she was starting to think it had to be, why else would someone try to destroy the body?—but she didn't know how or where the murder had taken place.

All she had in front of her was the end result of what must have been a nasty crime, like the period at the end of a sentence. That's all she knew, and somehow she had to work backward and try to begin to make out the words that came before it: the people, the fight, the reasons, the actions that led to this small pile of bones lying on the ground in the cold air.

Dr. Pinkers had pulled a digital camera out of one of the many pockets that dotted his vest. He started at the head and was slowly taking shots, moving down the length of the body.

Interesting that the body had been placed so its head was toward the front of the boat. This placement showed a kind of care that made her wonder about the relationship between the victim and the killer. Or was it just habitual, done without thinking? Like putting a body on a bed; even in haste one would naturally put the head toward the head of the bed.

When Pinkers finished taking photos, he stepped away from the site and pocketed the camera.

He lifted an eyebrow and asked, "Did you say something about coffee?"

"Two thermoses," she told him. "Even brought a mug for you."

"Some coffee would be lovely. Don't let me drink too much or my hands start to shake, and that's not good in this line of work."

Claire pulled a mug out of the pack in the back of the car and filled it for him, then refilled her own. "How long do you think it's going to take you?"

He glanced back at the site. "This is almost as easy as it gets. The bones have been seared clean. And they've not been disorganized. The structure of the body is still there. I'll start by collecting the skull, and work down to the feet." He looked out over the lake. "In another hour or so the light should be very good here. That will make all this even easier."

"Are you seeing anything new?"

"All I can tell so far confirms my feeling of yesterday that these are the bones of a female human. The skull size, the width of the innominate bone."

"What bone is that?"

"Sorry—that partially comprises the pelvis, as I mentioned before. We used to depend on the skull to tell sex, but that's not proven to be as reliable. I will know more as soon as I remove all this to the lab."

"How soon?"

"I should be able to give you an approximation of age and a definitive answer on the sex within a day or two."

"That's great."

He lifted his head and shook it as if trying to keep an irritant away. "But I do have some sad news."

Claire was struck by the fact that he said "sad" rather than "bad," showing his compassion for this victim. "What?"

"I'm not sure she was dead when she was put in the boat."

CHAPTER 6

What Meg wouldn't have given for a shower. Work at the Harbor View had been hot and heavy that day, although making salads was her favorite station. If she had the time, each salad would be little works of art, but with this nice weather, the leaves at their absolute peak of color, it had been a mob scene at the restaurant, and the salads had looked instead like fallen leaves.

After shrugging out of her apron, she went into the bathroom and wiped herself down as well as she could, then undid her hair, grown long over the summer, and let it fall way below her shoulders. She imagined Andrew's hands in her hair and shivered.

Calm down, she told herself. You might not even like him. He might be a total jerk. After all, he was a soldier, and you don't even believe in war. Maybe that subject would come up right away, and whatever romance could have been possible would blow up in their faces.

With this thought, she promised herself she wouldn't bring up the war. At least, not tonight. She would watch herself and be on good behavior. Curt had been gone almost two months, and she was missing some male attention. Maybe she and Andrew could just have some fun, nothing serious.

Meg leaned in and put on some eye shadow. She didn't wear much makeup, but she thought a touch of shadow brought out her eyes, made them seem bigger and more mysterious or something.

She pinched her cheeks, fluffed her hair, wiped her mouth, smoothed her eyebrows and declared herself ready.

When she walked out the door, Andrew was waiting by his car. A slow smile came onto his open face when he saw her. He was even more attractive than she remembered.

She felt like she was seeing him for the first time. At the Burning Boat, it had been dark and she hadn't seen him face on. Here he stood in the sunlight, skinnier than she thought, leaning against a Jeep. She was amazed to see he was driving a real car, not a truck. All the guys in Pepin drove trucks. His vehicle was a Jeep Cherokee. Old, but it looked like a decent car. Clean. A point for him.

Andrew was wearing a black T-shirt and jeans. No tattoos showed. His hair looked wet, as if he had just showered. Wheat blond hair, wide blue eyes, a baseball cap in his hands he was playing with, nervously.

As soon as Meg walked down the steps, he pushed off the Jeep with his butt and smiled, tossing his hat in the air.

"Hey," he shouted, then added, "Meg," as if he was testing the taste of her name.

When she was standing in front of him, he crowned her with his hat, but courteously, almost royally.

"Hey, Andrew, you're right on time."

"The service drills that into you." He laughed as he opened the door for her. Meg slid in and noticed it didn't smell like he smoked. Another point in his favor. He was racking them up.

"You mentioned a hike," he said. "You still up for it?"

"Sure."

"Not too tired after work?" He pulled away from the curb and headed out to the highway.

"Not at all," she lied. The back of her legs always ached after seven hours standing on her feet, but she knew that a walk would make them feel better. "What do you think?"

"Yeah, sounds good. Haven't been to the Maiden Rock since high school. Then let's come back here for burgers at Ralph and Mary's. I haven't had one of theirs since I got back home."

"Perfect."

She looked down at his feet and noticed the big boots he was wearing. "Those your army boots?" she asked.

"Yup. I've walked a million miles in them. I'm so used to wearing them it feels funny if they're not on my feet."

"They look like they weigh a ton."

"Everything we wore in Afghanistan weighed a ton." He said it like he was talking about more than boots and gear.

Meg wanted to steer the conversation away from the war, so she asked the first question that came to her mind. "Did you work today?"

"No, it's my day off."

"I don't even know where you work."

"Oh, I thought you knew. I work with your mom. I'm a deputy at the sheriff's department."

"My mom?" Meg was having trouble taking this in. She was going out with a guy who worked with her mom. Not only had he been a soldier, but now he was a cop. This was starting to feel like a really bad idea. "No, I didn't know that."

"Does it matter?" he asked.

Meg shrugged, trying to sound easy. "I suppose not."

"You don't sound so sure."

"Kinda weird." She rested her head back and looked out the window. The leaves were coming down. The day was on the edge of warm, but soon it would turn cold and the trees would be bare. Hopefully by the time snow fell, she would be going to school in Madison.

"Well, I didn't think Claire was old enough to have a daughter your age. How old are you?"

Meg thought of lying, she really did, but then admitted. "Eighteen."

"Shit, no kidding. I'm sorry. I didn't mean to swear."

"Hey, these ears are not virgin. Not around my mom and dad." She looked over at him. "Is that a problem?"

"I had no idea. You seem much older."

"How old are you?"

"Twenty-six."

"Not that much difference."

He laughed. "Well, at least you're legal."

"Yeah, I can have sex, get married, but I can't drink. That's what's really weird."

"I know what you mean. You can be a soldier, kill someone, but you can't drink either. What's that about?"

Neither of them said anything for a while, absorbing this new information about each other. Meg was really starting to wonder if this date with Andrew was a good idea. She couldn't imagine what her mom was going to say. Andrew turned off the highway, and they drove up through the tall cottonwoods and black walnut trees that lined the bluffs, then came out on top in cornfields.

"At the next road, turn to the left, obviously toward the bluff. It's not marked or anything. But there's a parking lot," she told him.

"I don't think I would have found it on my own. Just looks like any old country road."

The parking lot was where the old farmhouse had been. Meg loved the enormous maple trees that must have sheltered the house, given it shade. In the country, you could always tell where the farmhouses had been for the troop of trees left behind.

Andrew leaned toward her. "Listen, this doesn't have to get serious or anything. Let's just have a good time."

"Sure. It's not a big deal, you know, about you working with my mom or anything." She smiled at him. She loved his dark blue eyes.

He reached out a hand and touched her hair.

She didn't know how it happened. One minute they were smiling, facing each other, and the next moment, Andrew had wrapped a hand around her neck and pulled her close. She fell into him and their mouths came together.

So this is what it's like to kiss a man, she thought, no hesitation, no uncertainty. Just pure desire. When he touched her, it was as if all the doors in her body flew open. He came at her so hungry, she had felt no urge to resist. All she wanted to do was give him what he wanted. If she could.

❧

"I'm sure the boyfriend knows something," Amy said as she crawled into bed next to John. All she could see of him was his head peeking out above the quilt. "Hey, give me some covers."

"No talking about work. That's the rule, remember. Once we hit the bed, all talk of crime and punishment ceases. Come over here and get some covers if you want them." He held the quilt open for her.

She slid in next to him and noticed he wasn't wearing anything. That usually meant something. "I won't talk about work, but I just want it duly noted that I don't trust that boyfriend of poor

Tammy Lee. I wonder if she's really missing. I think she's run away. I wouldn't blame her. He seems like a creep. I'm going over to talk to her parents tomorrow. Didn't have a chance today."

"I can see I'm going to have to try drastic measures," John said and then pushed her down on the pillow and nuzzled her neck. His hands wrapped around her, then moved downward. Suddenly, he pulled back. "What're you wearing?"

"My flannel PJs."

He pulled back and looked down at her. "Flannel? Already? It's not winter. It's barely cold out."

"Well, maybe I wouldn't have to wear them if you were more generous with the covers."

He started to unbutton her top. "I'll keep you warm."

"So if it turns out that the boyfriend had something to do with her missing, I want you to be my witness that I suspected him all along."

He opened up her pajama top and wrapped his arms around her. He stretched out on top of her. "Warm enough?"

"Mmm," she said. Amy could feel his heart beating in her own chest. Like they were one creature.

"I know some ways to make things even a little hotter," he murmured.

❧

Rich fell asleep right after they had made love. Not so unusual for him, but for some reason, tonight Claire wanted him to be awake next to her as she was worrying about so many things: the sheriff, his job, the bones, her daughter. Somehow she felt shaken by life lately, like something really bad was going to happen and it was going to rip everything she knew apart.

She twitched and turned, sticking a foot out from under the covers, then pulling it back in, lying on one side, then shifting to the other. No position was comfortable, no temperature felt right. Thoughts pulsed through her head with a dangerous energy. There was no gentle drifting to sleep.

This unease was unusual for her these days. Since she had moved through menopause, Claire had reclaimed her previous easy sleep patterns, maybe sleeping a little less, but falling asleep quickly and waking up with the alarm, not the middle-of-the-night sweats.

What was getting to her? She had had bad anxiety years ago, after her husband had been killed, but then she'd seemed to get over it, be able to rock and roll with the best of them.

Claire thought her anxiety had to do with seeing the bones. There had been something so vulnerable about them. Lying in the ashes, bereft of the protection of their skin, they seemed delicate and fragile.

For most of the day, she had sat on a log by the shore watching as Dr. Pinkers gently lifted bone after bone, putting them in individual plastic bags, labeling them. There was no hurrying him. Somehow his work felt sacred, the lifting of the bones, the naming of them. Maybe she should have left him to it, but she felt like she needed to be there—both for the legality of chain of possession and for the honoring of the dead.

But watching the doctor work with the bones made her feel like she had seen what was inside herself, just this delicate necklace of ivory trinkets, too insignificant to carry the weight of a body. How did one manage to continue to move in this world, day after day, carrying on?

CHAPTER 7

Claire hated waiting for the forensic evidence to come in. When Dr. Pinkers left, the bones all safely packed in bags and then tucked into a foam container, he said he'd call her as soon as he knew anything. When she pushed him and asked when that might be, he squinted his eyes as if looking far off into the future. "I'll know something before the week's out."

She sat at her desk, not really waiting for the phone to ring but hoping it might, and at the same time getting some of her mountains of paperwork done. While Annette had suggested she move into Sheriff Talbert's office, that felt too uncomfortable— she told the secretary just to route all his calls her way.

There was always this weird lag time that happened after the very beginning of an investigation. On the first day there was the franticness of securing the site, interviewing witnesses, taking photos, gathering evidence. Then they would be done, and all the bits that they had pulled together would go off to the experts. She so wished it was like it was on TV, that it would take only as long as a commercial break for the information to come back to them.

The forensics were especially important, as they had a body with no name, no identity at all. No story. Wasn't that the worst of it? No sense of what had happened to this person?

Then there was the missing woman—Tammy Lee Johansen. Amy knew her from high school, said she was a bit of a flake, wouldn't be surprised if she was just out partying. Still, they had to take the report seriously. And what if she turned out to be the bones?

Claire looked down at her hands, seeing the bones push up against the skin more than they used to do when she was younger. Her nails were blunt cut so that she could work with them more easily. She wanted to get her hands dirty in this case, find out who those bones belonged to.

The bones were haunting her.

Andrew Stickler sauntered into the office, then came toward her desk, looking very happy with himself. She wondered what that was all about. He was generally pretty much a keep-your-head-down kind of guy. Behavior he'd probably learned in Afghanistan. Survival technique.

He stopped right by her desk and she looked up at him, couldn't help smiling back. "What's up with you?" she asked.

"I don't know if Meg had a chance to tell you last night. I know she got in kinda late," Andrew started, then stopped.

"What about Meg? I was asleep when she got home, but I heard her. What do you know about it?"

"Well, I was with her last night."

"Did you run into her some place?"

"No, we went out."

She sat up straight and asked more sharply than she intended, "You went out with Meg?"

"Yeah, it just happened. We met at that Burning Boat event. I didn't know who she was. Just hit it off. Then I found out she was your daughter. I hope you don't mind."

Claire didn't know what to say. Her daughter was eighteen years old, way too young to be going out with the likes of Andrew Stickler, who was mature in the ways of the world that she didn't want her daughter to know anything about, have anything to do with. At least, not yet. "I think I might mind."

"Oh."

"I mean, Andrew, what are you thinking? You're way too old for her. She's still a teenager."

"I didn't realize how young she was when I asked her out. I thought she was in her twenties."

"I think you need to think twice about this, Andrew. She's not even going to be here for much longer. She's going off to school in Madison." Claire hated that she was saying this, but the words came out of their own volition. "She's not ready for someone like you."

"What does that mean?" Andrew's body tightened up, his shoulders raised, his voice sharp.

"Andrew, it's nothing against you at all. My concerns are all about Meg. She's a young eighteen. She's hardly been away from home. You've traveled, you've seen things. My God, you've been to war."

"Yes, I have. I've served my country. And now I'm home, trying to find my way in this new life. Meg will have to decide. I'd like to see her again, but if she doesn't think she's ready for someone like me, then she can tell me that."

Claire watched him walk away. That had not gone well. Somehow she had said all the wrong things. She'd have to talk to Meg and make her see that going out with Andrew Stickler was probably not a good idea right now. Maybe later, after she had gone to college, met some guys her own age, done some living of her own.

Right now, Andrew just seemed like too much man for Meg. Wasn't a mother's job to protect her daughter from the likes of such men? Who knows what he had seen or done in Afghanistan?

の

Andrew stood on the edge of the woods by the county building and smoked a cigarette. It was the one he allowed himself every day. He had gone into the service a nonsmoker, but that changed as soon as he hit the ground in Afghanistan. Everyone smoked. Babies there smoked, as far as he knew. Once he got home he quit. It was hard, but he didn't want the memories that came with lighting up a cigarette. Then, after a couple of months without a single butt, he started smoking a single cigarette a day. Maybe so he wouldn't forget. Maybe just so he could taste that world again.

He knew Watkins was right. He had no business going out with her daughter. Meg knew nothing of the world he lived in, had lived in, had pushed so deep into him that he wasn't sure he would ever come out of it.

But she was like a peach. The sweetest, ripest, best-smelling peach he had ever tasted. And she wanted to be picked. He could feel that energy all along her skin. They had come close last night. Pulling himself away from her was one of the hardest things he had ever had to do—but once he had felt where they were headed, he had scrambled out of the car and pulled her out for their walk.

Things had calmed down then. They had sat on the very edge of the Maiden Rock and watched the barges coming up the river, the cars sailing by below on the ribbon of the road, and the trains threading through the trees. It had been good for him, sitting and talking about things that normal people talked about on a date— music, school, dreams. The way life used to be.

Meg was a very smart kid. Seemed quite determined. She claimed she didn't want to be a cop like her mom—she apologized, not like him either. She thought maybe a lawyer.

"So like a super cop?" he had teased her.

"You think?"

"In a way. Just heavier artillery."

She had laughed, tossed her long dark hair, and said, "Oh, yeah, you with the military metaphors."

"Bother you?"

She shrugged. "It's different."

"Don't you know any guys from school that went into the service?"

"Yeah, I know 'em, but I didn't hang out with them."

That statement hung in the air between them. He held out his hand to her. "I'm hungry. Let's go get a burger."

The rest of the evening had been light, fizzy almost. Andrew wanted to sit across from her in a booth and watch her eyes catch the bar light forever and a day. Truly.

He drove her back to her car parked by the Harbor View and got out to open the door for her before they could kiss again. Too dangerous.

But she had grabbed him at her car door and they had sealed the night with one more kiss. There had been no talk of seeing each other again. There was no question of that, he was sure. He could hardly keep from calling her right now, standing smoking a cigarette and looking at the woods.

He was flicking his cigarette off toward the trees when an arm grabbed him and swung him around.

There was no time for thought, just action.

Andrew rounded on the man and slammed a fist into him so hard he could feel the shudder of the body through his own.

Then he remembered where he was and stared down at the young man crumpled at his feet.

"I'm sorry," he said, gulping in air, shaking. He reached down to help the guy to his feet.

"What the hell?" The guy wouldn't take his hand, crouched on the ground. He was about Andrew's age, and wore a flannel shirt and jeans. His dark hair was long and pulled back in a ponytail. He stared at Andrew like he was a madman. "Why'd you do that?"

"You startled me," Andrew tried to explain.

"So you slug me?"

Andrew didn't know what to say. They warned him something like this might happen, but he hadn't quite believed it. "Jumpy. Just out of the service."

The man stood, his face tightened. "You're Andrew Stickler."

"Yes, how did you know that?"

"I'm Terry. You're the guy I'm looking for." Then he pulled his arm back and slugged Andrew in the chest.

Andrew doubled over and staggered, trying not to fall. His breath came in wheezes. "What?"

"Where's Tammy Lee?" Terry yelled at him.

Two deputies who had been walking out of the county offices came running up and grabbed Terry's arms, holding him back.

"What're you talking about?" Andrew gasped out, straightening up and breathing deep. "What about Tammy?"

"She was supposed to see you, and then she went missing."

Andrew shook his head. "She never showed up. I didn't think anything of it. It's so like her."

"Well, she's been gone for over two days now, and you might be the last person she talked to."

"She's missing?"

"Yeah, like you don't know. You don't fool me." Terry tried to shake free of the deputies. "Whatever happened to her is all your fault. You just wouldn't leave her alone."

"What're you talking about?"

"Even after she broke up with you, you kept bothering her."

Andrew shook his head. He wasn't going to argue with Terry. He obviously had concocted his own vision of the world, or Tammy Lee had lied to him. "Terry, I'm sure she'll show up. She always does."

Terry stepped back, but kept his guard up. "If she doesn't show up, I know where you are. I know you're the one responsible."

❧

"This isn't the first time she's done this." Mrs. Johansen stood at her kitchen counter, smoking a cigarette.

Amy was standing in their living room. There had been no offer of coffee, not even the offer of a chair.

"So you're not worried about your daughter?"

"Naw, she's been mighty prickly lately. The wedding's got her all in a fluster. She'll be back in her own good time. For a few years, she lived in Minneapolis. She's probably up there now, staying with some friends. I'm sure she'll be back in time for work."

"Her fiancé Terry seems pretty upset."

"He's an excitable guy. He better get used to Tammy's ways or he's going to have a rough ride."

"When is the wedding?"

"Right before Thanksgiving. It's coming up quick. Tammy's been saving up money so she could have the kind of wedding she's always dreamed of—you know, the big white dress, the five bridesmaids, the whole nine yards. We can't help her out much, so she's saving her own money."

"When did you last see her?"

"Had to be Friday. I mean, she's twenty-six years old, for God's sake. I don't keep track of her. She works odd hours, she stays at Terry's most of the time."

"Since a missing persons report has been filed, I need to follow up on this. I'd like to ask you some questions."

"Who filed the report?"

"Terry, her fiancé."

"Oh, like I said, he's just a little nervous. He's always checking up on her. Tammy'll be back."

"Well, I do need to finish filling the report out. I have some questions I'd like to ask you. May I sit down?"

"It's a free country."

Sometimes Amy wondered if it was. She sat down on a stool at the counter and pulled out the missing persons report that Terry had filled out. "What was she wearing when you saw her last?"

"Jeans. Can't really remember. Some kind of shirt. It's been so warm. Probably a T-shirt. Nothing special."

"Any distinctive jewelry?"

"She would be wearing the engagement ring that Terry got her—you know, the usual . . . a small diamond, think she said it was half a carat. Probably some earrings, hoops."

"I'd like to talk to her sister. Could you give me her phone number?"

Mrs. Johansen rattled the number off. "Yeah, talk to Bria. She might know more than me. They're real close."

"I knew Bria."

"Yeah."

"She went to school with me."

"I thought you looked familiar."

"Where's she living now?"

"Hastings. She's teaching school there."

"Good for her."

"Yeah, Bria was always the studious one. Not like Tammy. Tammy was our happy kid, goofing off all the time. Just wanted to have fun, like that Madonna song." Mrs. Johansen sounded uncertain for the first time. "She can get a little wild, but I'm sure she'll turn up soon."

CHAPTER 8

The call Claire had been waiting for all day came in just as she was leaving work. She had almost walked out the main door, but the secretary caught her as she was heading home.

Claire walked back to her desk to take the call, pulling out paper and pen to take notes.

A man's precise voice came over the line. "Just as I thought. That pelvic bone told the story."

"Dr. Pinkers?" Claire checked.

"Yes, sorry. I've got some preliminary information for you. Thought I should call you with it."

"What do you know?" Claire started drawing the shape of the pelvic bone. In her doodle, it looked like a big bow.

"As I had surmised yesterday at the scene on the lake, I feel very confident in saying that the bones belonged to a young woman."

Claire couldn't help thinking that "belonged" was an odd word to use about something that actually made up a part of the person. And the use of the past tense was also disconcerting. "Can you estimate the age?"

"Well, I say young, advisedly. At this time, I would put her age between twenty and thirty. Her bones had fully matured and there is no evidence of any arthritis or osteoporosis yet."

"Okay, that helps."

"But I'm afraid that you do have some sort of case on your hands. Unfortunately, the back of the skull had sustained some trauma. I would say that it was hit with some sort of blunt instrument—a board, a bat—which causes hairline fractures throughout the surface of the skull. The impact, rather than being focused on one spot, is generalized across the base of the skull." He paused for a moment, then continued. "What I saw was a depressed skull fracture, which is comminuted, with broken portions of the bone displaced inward. The way I read it, it was done with a lot of force. This was a bad fracture and put a lot of pressure on the brain."

Claire sank down into her chair. "And do you still think that she was alive? That she was, in fact, burned to death?"

"I'm afraid I do, but the good news is that with this kind of fracture I doubt very much that she would have been conscious. I suppose whoever put her there might even have thought she was dead. With that kind of trauma to the brain, there is a very good chance that she was not cognizant of what was happening to her."

"I hate to think . . . ." Claire said.

"I will continue to gather my notes and will send you a full report by the end of the week, but I felt that you should know this as soon as I was comfortable with my findings. This will give you something to go on."

"Listen, we've got a missing person report just filed—a young woman about this age. Are you able to check dental records against the teeth you have?"

"Yes, if you can find out who her dentist was and get her most recent dental records, I can see how they compare to her remaining teeth."

"All right. Sounds like a plan. I'll locate the dentist and talk to you tomorrow." Claire took a deep breath. "Thank you for getting back to me so quickly."

Right after Claire hung up, Amy walked into the department. She headed Claire's way.

"What's the news?" Claire asked.

Amy slouched over, leaning on the corner of Claire's desk. "She didn't show up for work."

"Our missing woman?"

"Yup, Tammy Lee was supposed to work the evening shift at the Pump and Dump. Fran claims that she's been real reliable. Her mom told me that she has done a walkabout before. But also that lately she's been working really hard to pay for her wedding. Which would make it unlikely that she'd skip work and not at least call."

"Got some news on our bones."

"And?"

"Woman in her twenties, that's what the good doctor thinks so far."

"Hmm."

"Can you find out who Tammy Lee's dentist is?"

❦

"Hey, Grandma."

A thin old woman looked out at him from the doorway, her eyes squinted in a glare. Her gray hair was pulled back in a thin ponytail, and she was wearing a faded blue sweatshirt with a big daisy on the front. "Who are you?"

"Don't you know me? It's Dougie." If he hadn't been standing at her door, he wouldn't have recognized her, either. Grandma

Schubert looked so much smaller than he remembered, and she looked about twenty years older than the last time he saw her, which had only been about five years ago. Before Mom and her had had the big fight. He couldn't even remember what they fought about. But he knew they hadn't talked since.

"Dougie. I haven't seen you in forever. Come on in. What're you doing here?" She shuffled back and let him enter her house.

He walked into the kitchen. The place looked clean, hadn't changed much since last time he was there, but it didn't smell so good. Like someone had forgotten to empty the kitty litter box for a couple months or so. "Just thought I'd stop by. I'm going to see a buddy of mine from the army. He lives pretty close to here and you were right on the way."

"You were in the army?"

"Yeah, fought over there with the jinglies in Afghanistan for two long tours of duty."

"Way over there?"

"That's where they sent me."

She walked closer to him and touched his face. "You're not old enough to go to war, are you?"

"I'm twenty-two, Grandma. You can join the army when you're seventeen and a half."

"Would you like a cup of coffee?"

What he really wanted to do was fall asleep on her couch, but he figured he better talk to her for a while. "Sure. You got any grub?"

"I could make you some toast. With peanut butter."

"Sounds good, Grandma. How've you been?"

She wasn't walking so good, more like a shuffle. Didn't help that she was wearing big furry slippers. She put two pieces of bread in the toaster, then turned and leaned on the counter, her arms folded. "I'm not so good, Dougie. I got that cancer. Been eating me up."

"Really? You got cancer?"

"Yeah. They've been giving me chemo, but it's worse than the cancer." Suddenly, she turned sharp and said, "But don't you go telling your ma. I don't want her to come sniveling around here just because I'm sick. She's not getting this house or anything from me."

"I won't tell her."

Grandma smiled and he could see what she used to look like for a moment. "You're a good kid, Dougie. Always were a good kid. How is your ma?"

"She's okay. Me and her kinda had a fight, too. I'm not doing so well myself since I came back. Don't seem to wanta do anything."

"You got bad nerves?" The toast popped up and she slathered it with butter, then peanut butter.

"I guess you could call it that. It's got some fancy name—posttraumatic syndrome, you know how those doctors are." He tried to keep the thoughts from coming, thoughts of the life outside the wire, deep in the suck of it all.

When she put the plate of toast down in front of him, something in him started to crack. He wanted to go back to when he was ten and he would come to visit, and she would mess up his hair and tell him to wash his hands before he ate. He wanted it to be before all the stuff he had seen and couldn't get out of his head.

"You eat that now, Dougie."

"Thanks, looks good." He took a bite, chewed it slowly, then swallowed it. His head fell forward and he started to cry. "I don't know what to do, Grandma. I don't seem to be able to come back."

∓

"Is this Bria Johansen?" Amy asked when a woman answered the phone. She had a clear picture of seeing Bria at their five-year high school reunion. She had worn a long black sweater with a fur collar that had seemed incredibly stylish to Amy, who had thrown a light blue cotton sweater on over her jeans. She had made Amy feel as awkward as she had always felt in school.

"Yes, this is she."

Amy recognized the voice—breathy, but rather sophisticated. Hard to believe that she had gone to school in Pepin County. "This is Deputy Sheriff Amy Peterson. I'm calling about your sister."

"Hey, Amy. My mom said you stopped by. She hasn't shown up yet? I wish I could say I'm surprised, but this is not unusual for Tammy."

"Well, she didn't show up for work and her fiancé Terry is getting quite worried. Can I ask you a few questions?"

"Sure, glad to help."

"Both you and your mom have said that she's done this before. Why? What does she do, exactly?"

"Well, Tammy Lee likes to party and she has a lot of friends. In Minneapolis, all over the place. Sometimes she'll go out with friends and Mom won't hear from her for a few days."

"Does she do drugs?"

"Probably. She and I don't talk about that stuff much, we don't hang out with the same people, but I've seen her when she seems kinda messed up. I wouldn't say she has a problem, but I doubt she says no to anything that's offered."

"Has anything been going on recently that would cause her to disappear?"

"Well," Bria sighed on the other end. "I hate to tell on her, but you know she's getting married soon, right?"

"Yes, your mom said before Thanksgiving."

"Tammy Lee and Terry have been going out for a while. He popped the question early this summer. They picked a date and everything. Then Andrew Stickler came back to town."

"Andrew? Why, I work with Andrew."

"I heard he got a job with the sheriff. Anyhow, Tammy said that he'd been trying to see her and all. I don't think she ever got over Andrew. So now she's having mixed feelings about Terry."

"You mean you think that she might call off the wedding?"

"She's been hinting at something like that, but she's so changeable. One day she'll say she can't stand Terry, the next she's buying her wedding dress. I didn't think too much of her indecision. At one time she and Andrew were real tight, but then when he left, well, Tammy Lee's not one to wait around."

"So she broke up with him?"

"I guess she texted him to say it was over. Isn't that awful. Here he is, halfway around the world. Sounds worse than a Dear John letter to me. But I was surprised when she did it, because she was pretty whipped on him. Even after she claimed they were through, she would still talk about him. She got real patriotic and everything. She threatened to join the service herself. Thank goodness she didn't take it that far. Although maybe the military would have been a good thing for her, teach her some life lessons."

"When was the last time you talked to your sister?"

"I think it was Thursday night. Yeah, it was and now I remember, she said she was meeting Andrew. She sounded real excited. She said she was going to meet him at that big fire they do down at the lake. What's it called again?"

"Burning Boat."

"Yeah, she said she was looking forward to watching it all go up in flames."

CHAPTER 9

Claire stared at the x-ray that Dr. Pinkers had slapped up on the lightboard. Ghostly teeth shone out of a black background.

This was why she had driven the dental x-rays to Dr. Pinkers' lab herself, even though it was an hour away. She wanted to see how he did this, she wanted to know how he matched them or didn't. Plus she wanted to know the news right away, to know if they had found the person the bones belonged to.

"Very good," Dr. Pinkers said. "This full-mouth x-ray should give us all the information we need." He pointed back toward the table she was standing by. "There's our comparison."

Claire moved in closer and looked down at the teeth and jawbones that had been gathered from the burn site. While there was some darkening of the bones, the teeth remained fairly clean. Or maybe Pinkers had cleaned them. "I'm amazed how good they look. Doesn't seem like the fire hurt them at all."

"Oh yeah, teeth last through almost anything. They're the hardest part of the human body, the last thing to go. That little fire didn't come close to destroying them. They can last in blast furnaces up to two thousand degrees Fahrenheit."

He walked up to the x-ray, took off his glasses and stood inches away from it, staring with the intensity of a creature ready to pounce. "These are going to serve the purpose." He pointed at the x-ray with his glasses. "These are decent x-rays, which will make my work easy."

"Can you always get a positive ID?"

"Not always. If we have a strong suspicion, if the teeth have been damaged in some way and we're not sure, we can extract DNA from the pulp and make a positive ID using that method."

Pinkers went back to staring at the x-ray. Claire stared with him. She could see the eye sockets floating like ghoulish orbs above the flattened jawbone—the teeth were lined up like a rock wall with the roots stretching out above and below them. The whitest objects on the screen were the bright almost-twinkle of the fillings. She counted eight white splots, mainly in the back teeth.

"What exactly are you looking for?" she asked. "What do you concentrate on to do the match?"

"I study the arrangement of the teeth, the fillings, and other dental work. I count the teeth to see if any are missing. I look for any anomalies—broken teeth, noticeable crookedness. Every mouth is different. Even the bite marks are recognizably different."

"I know about that. I've worked on cases where we've had to take an imprint of a bite mark from an assailant."

"Yes, that can work."

"What do you think?"

Dr. Pinkers circled the x-ray with his finger. "Looks like she had braces. Her teeth are pretty regular and evenly laid out. But she has a lot of fillings. Must have eaten candy when she was a kid."

"Who didn't."

"I don't really care for candy myself."

Somehow she was not surprised. Claire stepped back and watched him. He continued to look at the x-ray from very close range, his eyes traveling up and down the film, his mouth moving with no sound coming out as if he was holding a private conversation with himself. He snuffled through his nose; he nodded his head; he turned and put his glasses back on.

"I would say that the teeth that we have found definitely match the teeth in this x-ray. What did you say her name was?"

"Tammy Lee Johansen."

"And her family filed a missing persons?"

"Her fiancé."

"Sad. She will not be getting married. But at least they can bury her, knowing what has happened."

"Not everything. Not who did this."

Doctor Pinkers stared at Claire in the same way that he had been looking at the x-ray, close and concentrated. "My work is done. That is your job."

☙

The Johansens lived just on the outskirts of the small town of Arkansaw, only about a ten minute drive from Durand. Pretty country, rolling hills, with a creek running right through town.

By the time Claire got to their house, the sun was setting and she could see the ghostly light of a TV flickering in what she guessed was the living room. Claire knocked on the front door, staring right at an orange pumpkin head that had been hung at eye level. Yes, Halloween was on its way.

A woman with straw blond hair and a cigarette hanging out of her mouth came to the door. She looked to be in her forties and dressed like she was in her twenties: tight jeans, tight top with writing on it, and her hair pulled close to her head.

She took the cigarette out of her mouth and said, "Yeah," then did a double take when she took in the uniform. The woman sucked in her breath. "Tammy Lee?" she asked.

"Mrs. Johansen?" Claire asked.

The woman nodded, but didn't step back inside the house. Then she said, "Bobby, you can call me Bobby."

"Is your husband here?"

"He's not home yet. What about Tammy Lee?"

"May I come inside?"

"You're going to tell me bad news." Bobby still didn't move. She held her cigarette like it would burn her.

"I'm sorry," Claire started.

Bobby crumpled. She jabbed the cigarette into her jeans and then fell to a heap on the floor. "Not Tammy Lee."

Claire reached down and tried to help her up. "Let's go inside and talk."

"I don't want to hear it. I don't want to know what happened to her. Can't you go away?" Anger and fear mixed in the woman's throaty voice.

If it were only that easy, Claire thought. She got Bobby on her feet, took her into the house, and sat her on the couch. Because there was no chair close by, Claire perched on the end of the coffee table. The TV was going on about the specials at the Furniture Barn.

"I can't tell you how sorry I am. I know how hard this is, but I must tell you that we are quite sure that your daughter is dead. I've just come from a positive identification of bones found in Fort St. Antoine as belonging to your daughter."

"Bones? What're you talking about?"

Claire hated to have to tell her about the bones. She reached out and put a hand on the woman's knee. "Tammy Lee was knocked unconscious and then put into the Burning Boat. Her bones were found in the ashes."

Then the screaming started. Bobby opened her mouth and a high piercing shriek came out that wavered, then went on even louder. Claire couldn't stand it. She stood up and went into the kitchen to get Bobby something to drink and find something to wipe her face.

Even though Claire didn't want to hear the screams, she respected them. They were the last gasp of motherhood, trying desperately to get a child back, trying to scream her back into existence. When they stopped, Bobby would have to face the truth. So Claire let her scream a while longer, then walked back into the living room to tell Bobby what she knew.

⁊

Meg sat at the kitchen counter, cutting up carrots for Rich. She had to keep her hands busy while she was waiting for the phone to ring. She hadn't heard from Andrew all day yesterday, and now most of today had passed as well. Curt and she had always talked every day when they were a steady thing. At least a check-in call. It didn't have to be very long. But since that was the only relationship she had been in, she wasn't sure what was normal, especially with an older guy.

"You know, I went on a date the other night," Meg mentioned casually as she handed the bowl of carrot coins to Rich.

"So that's why you were out so late." Rich dumped the carrots in the pheasant broth. "Anyone we know?"

"Mom knows him," Meg said, not sure she was ready to tell Rich she was going out with a deputy.

"I hope that doesn't mean he's a felon."

Meg laughed. "Hardly. He was in the army over in Afghanistan."

Rich looked at her. "That's tough. How's he doing?"

"He seems good. He's in super good shape."

Rich laughed. "I don't need to know about that."

Meg giggled. It was nice to talk about Andrew with someone. Odd how she could often talk more easily about things with Rich than her mom. "He said the countryside was really wild and dangerous. He said the mountains were so rugged it looked like someone had taken really long fingernails and just dragged them down the side, making these deep ravines."

"Did he see much action?"

"Not that he's mentioned. But I think he was in a difficult spot, some sort of outpost in the hills."

Just then her mom came stomping in the door. Meg checked her out to see what kind of mood she was in.

Claire had her mouth clamped shut, the stomps a little harder than necessary, not good signs.

"We waited on dinner for you," Meg said as her mom flung her jacket on a chair. "You look tired."

"I had to go to Eau Claire to get some forensic testing done. But it was worth it. We found out who the bones belong to. Someone from around here, I'm sorry to say. Then I had to go tell the family. It's never any fun to get that news. I'm glad to know, but sorry it's someone from our community."

"Who was it?" Meg asked.

Her mom looked at her intently. "Tammy Lee Johansen. The name mean anything to you?"

"Nope. Should it?"

"She went out with someone you know."

"Curt? I don't think so."

"No, someone more recent." Claire looked up at Meg and pinned her with a hard stare. "Someone you're going out with now."

Meg had a bad feeling. She had meant to tell her mom about Andrew, but she hadn't felt like the time was right yet. Her mom didn't look very happy. "I was going to tell you."

"When? After the whole county knew?"

"Whoa, let me in on this." Rich pulled a beer out of the fridge and handed it to her mom. "What's this about, Claire?"

Her mom took the beer, but just held it in her lap. Another not so good sign. "Do you know who Meg went out with the other night?"

"She was just telling me about it—but she hadn't divulged his name yet."

"Andrew Stickler. The new deputy."

Rich nodded. "Well, that's good. Then she'll be safe, won't she?"

"I'm not so sure about that. I haven't talked to Andrew yet since I found out that the bones were Tammy Lee's, but he has some explaining to do. Like where he was Friday and Saturday night."

This was not sounding good, but at least Meg could clear up one of those nights. "I know where he was Saturday. I saw him at the Burning Boat event. That's where I met him."

"Lord," her mom said. "So he was at the Burning Boat. I don't like any of this one bit."

"What? Explain."

"I can't talk to you about this, Meggy. But I don't want you to see Andrew until I get a few things straightened out."

"Why not?"

"Because it's too complicated."

"Tell me."

"Meg, I can't. I will when I can. You have to just do what I ask you to do."

"Mom, I'm almost nineteen. You can't treat me like a child anymore."

"Yes, but you're still living in my home and I'm the boss."

"Mom," Meg whined in spite of herself. She knew her mom never responded to that.

Claire stepped forward and took her by the shoulders. Her eyes were fierce and sad at the same time. "Just give me a day or two. I don't mean to come down on you so hard, but this is important. I'm asking you to not see him until I tell you it's okay. Can you do that?"

Meg nodded, and also decided it might be time to call Andrew herself.

こ

"Doug, I made some dinner. You hungry?"

He rolled over and tried to figure out where he was. The wallpaper looked familiar—small roses with twining vines. It made him happy. The voice was his grandmother's. For a time, he was safe.

"Yup," he said and sat up. His head felt like it had a weight attached to it and his hands were shaky on his knees. "Give me a sec."

"Take your time. Nothing fancy. Just grilled cheese and tomato soup out of a can."

He wondered what time it was. Grandma always ate on the early side. Farm time, they called it. It was dark in the room he was in, but he could see sunshine through the open door. She walked back into the kitchen, and he stood up.

The room stayed quiet. He stood still for a moment, getting his bearings. He used to be able to jump out of a dead sleep and be ready to shoot someone. Now he could hardly walk, let alone pee, which was what he really needed to do.

He made his way out of the room, blinking in the sunlight, and then shuffled down the hallway to the bathroom. A cat wound around his legs, but he just let it. Didn't hurt nothing.

After he peed, he went to the sink and washed his hands. How had they gotten so dirty? All he'd been doing was driving.

Then he lifted his head up and looked at his face. Wasn't good. Eyes rimmed with red, pouchy looking. Beard a few days old, never amounted to much. Hair growing out. Had to be a good four inches long, in his eyes.

Even though he wanted to get done what he had come to do, maybe he'd take a day and recoup. Clean up a bit. Hang with Grandma. Go walk out on the land that his grandfather had farmed, even though it was now sold to the neighbors.

He knew where his grandpa had kept the gun in the barn. He'd check and make sure it was still there. There was no hurry. Andrew wasn't going anywhere. He'd checked on him when he came through Durand, driven by Andrew's house, talked to people in a bar, gotten info out of the girlfriend.

Not quite as pretty as in her picture, but not bad. She said she and Andrew had broken up but were getting back together. She bragged about him—said he was a cop now. Which made it all just perfect. A cop, protecting and defending his community. Too bad he hadn't been able to do that in Afghanistan.

Doug didn't mind waiting. Things had been set in motion.

His mission was always there in front of him, pulling him along.

Maybe he was afraid to do it, 'cause then what would he have to keep going?

CHAPTER 10

On her drive to work, Claire tried to figure out how she would approach Andrew. She liked the guy. He was a great addition to the sheriff's department—knowledgeable, levelheaded, knew the territory, which often came in handy. He was already accepted by the community, welcomed, in fact. By most, he was seen as a hero.

But true heroes are few and far between. And they often came with fatal flaws. She had heard about the contretemps he had had in the parking lot with Terry Whitman, although the deputies who saw it had assured her that Andrew hadn't been at fault.

Claire tried to pull her thoughts away from the conversation she would try to have with Andrew as soon as she saw him this morning. The fall weather was holding, cool and crisp, but sunny. The leaves were just past their peak of color, swathing the bluffs in shawls of muted paisleys. But Claire felt in her bones what was pushing behind all this glory—winter, the season of the dead. Beautiful in its own spare way, but definitely monochromatic. She tried to breathe in the color, store it in her body for those bleak days to come.

As she turned up Highway 25, she drove through rolling farmland, away from the Mississippi and along the Chippewa River. The grasses and hay fields were golden and glowing in the early morning sun. These days, she met the sun on the way to work. Soon it would not appear until after she had arrived at the Government Center.

Claire was also trying to figure out all the reasons that it bothered her that Meg was going out with Andrew—aside from the fact that his ex-girlfriend had been murdered. She just thought there was something wrong with her young daughter going out with a man who worked with her mother, who was her colleague. Then there was Andrew's age, not to mention his experiences. If Meg were thirty, Andrew being eight years older wouldn't matter so much, but at her current age the life experience was much greater. Then there was the factor of him being an ex-soldier. Claire had such mixed feelings about that. Some of the very things that made her want him as a deputy worked against him going out with Meg—the atrocities he might have seen, might have been a part of. The psychological problems that the experience of being in a war zone carry with it.

The good news was that Meg wasn't going to be around much longer, which was also the bad news. How would she let her darling daughter go? Send her off into the world with all the good blessings she could manage.

First things first. Find out where Andrew was Friday night. That would settle most of her worries, and that was her job. Whatever happened to Tammy Lee had probably happened on Friday night.

Claire pulled her vehicle into the Government Center lot and looked over the squad cars. Seemed like Andrew was still here. Good. She wanted to get their conversation over with so she could get on with the day.

The more she thought about it, the more she doubted he could have had anything to do with it. Even though she knew it was silly to think such a thing, Andrew had such an open face, was still such a farm boy . . . how could he have killed anyone?

❧

Andrew was sitting hunched over his desk trying to fill out a form when he saw that Claire Watkins had walked in. He felt her eyes on him, but he didn't look up.

"Hey, Stickler," she called out. "Meet me in the sheriff's office when you finish with that."

He slapped his hand down on the form and looked up at her. Might as well get it over with—whatever it was. He knew she wasn't happy about him seeing Meg, which was one of the reasons why he hadn't called her daughter again. Maybe he shouldn't be seeing the girl. He stood up. "Right now would be fine. I'm tired of trying to figure these forms out. They're worse than what we had to fill out in the service."

Andrew followed her into the sheriff's office and watched as she took one of the two chairs that were sitting in front of the desk. He sat down in the other one. She didn't seem ready to claim her job as sheriff. He understood. Might seem too disrespectful, or might be too hard to give it up once the sheriff was back on the job. He didn't know Claire that well, and she was a hard woman to read.

"Yup," he said, folding his hands on his belt.

"I have some bad news."

So many things flashed through his head: he was fired, Meg had gotten hurt, they had found out what had happened in Afghanistan, Claire didn't want him to see her daughter. He managed to ask, "What?"

"Tammy Lee Johansen. You knew her, right?"

"Yes, we knew each other in high school and went out a few years ago. Before I left town."

"She's dead. You heard about the bones we found in the fire. They've been identified as hers."

He didn't really feel much and he knew his face was blank. Tammy Lee had been fun, a great girl to hang out with before you left to fight for your country, a party girl. But he hadn't known her that well, really. Her death made him fear something more. What if it was all coming back to get him?

"How?" he asked.

"Well, it appears she was hit on the head and then put in the bottom of the boat before it was set on fire."

"Any ideas?" he asked.

Claire stared at him, then asked, "Where were you Friday night?"

She couldn't really be asking him that, suspecting he had something to do with the murder. Stay calm, he told himself. He had to think. "At home. I'm staying with my folks. We watched TV. They went to bed. I stayed up and watched until I fell asleep."

"That's all?"

"Yeah, nothing much happened," he said, but he remembered the two phone calls. The first from Tammy Lee, asking him to meet him at the Burning Boat. He had to tell Claire about that one. If not, she would find out some other way and it would look very bad for him. "Except I did get a call. From Tammy Lee. We had run into each other at a bar a few days earlier and she had wanted to talk. We decided to meet at the Burning Boat."

"You didn't see her before then?"

"No. I wondered when she didn't show, but that was like Tammy Lee. Couldn't really count on her."

"You mind if I talk to your parents?" she asked as a courtesy.

"No, that's fine. Of course. Check with them."

"I'm sorry to have to do this, Andrew," she said. "Also, as a favor to me, would you not see Meg until we get this straightened out?"

Andrew didn't say anything right away. Not see Meg. The only person he had found comfort with since he had returned home. But why involve her with this whole mess. "Sure."

"She's leaving soon for college."

"I know," he said, and then thought he shouldn't have. Shouldn't reveal how much he knew about Meg already.

"Thanks," Claire said and stood.

Andrew stood and left the room. When he sat at his desk, he felt panic surge over him. He wrapped his hands together so they wouldn't shake. He would never get out of it. He hadn't told Claire about the second phone call, the one that came later, after his parents had gone to bed, from Doug.

That phone call had bothered him so much he had left the house and gone for a long walk. He had gone out without his coat or gloves or hat. He had walked in the darkness of the country roads and felt like he was back in Afghanistan, cold and tired and weary of something more than exhaustion, weary of the stink of scared men and his own fear that ate away his bones.

He had wished so hard that he could make everything right again. He didn't know what time he had stumbled back into the house.

❧

When Amy got the news from Claire that the bones were definitely Tammy Lee's, it didn't surprise her. But she was surprised by how matter-of-factly she took the news. Was she turning into such a cop that nothing got to her anymore? She hoped not.

"Would you go and talk to the boyfriend?" Claire asked, tapping a pencil on her desk, a new nervous habit Amy had noticed. "He might have been told the news by Tammy Lee's parents, but he deserves to know. See what he's up to, and how he reacts. He might well be our guy. Ask him to stick around."

"Sure, I'll head out right now."

"Did you know him at school?"

"Name sounds familiar, but he's probably a few years older than me."

"Ancient," Claire said, then smiled.

"When you're a teenager, it makes a difference."

"Tell that to my daughter."

"What?" Amy asked, wondering what this was about.

"Oh, nothing. She started dating a guy who's almost ten years older than her."

"John's older than me."

"But you're not a teenager."

"Meg hardly is anymore either."

"Whose side are you on?"

Amy laughed. "The side of the law. And your daughter's legal, whether you want her to be or not."

"Get out of here," Claire said sternly, but her eyes crinkled. "If we don't get something definite on how Tammy Lee died in the next twenty-four hours, I'm calling in some help."

Amy made a couple of calls and found out that Terry worked for the railroad. He'd be days on the road, then have time off. She called his number and he answered, but sounded barely awake. She simply said she'd be out to see him and hung up. She never liked to tell people about a death over the phone.

He lived out of town in a trailer parked in front of falling-down farmhouse. Amy got out of the squad car and stood for a few minutes, looking at the old house. It always made her sad to see the old houses sink into the ground.

Terry's trailer looked fairly respectable, and he had piled hay bales around the perimeter of the structure to winterize it. Looked goofy, but not a bad idea. Keep the winter winds from whistling under the floor.

She walked up to the door and rapped twice. Waiting, she heard someone moving around inside. As she started to knock again, the door was pulled open and a man with greasy brown hair and wearing a flannel shirt and jeans looked out at her. The clothes looked like they had just been pulled on.

"Sorry to wake you," she said.

"I don't care. What about Tammy Lee?" he said. "I'm worried sick."

"May I come in?" she asked.

He backed up and she stepped into his small space. Dirty dishes were stacked next to the small sink. A window wrapped around the eating area and there was a nice view down a field. A couple *Field & Stream* magazines sat on the fold-down table.

Terry didn't offer her a seat. He just stood staring at her.

"I'm so sorry to have to tell you this—but I'm afraid she's dead."

"How?"

"We have confirmation that the bones found at the burn site are Tammy Lee's."

He turned his back to her. He walked to the window and put his hands above the frame. "I can't believe it." He spit out the words.

"I'm sorry."

"We were going to be married. We had it all planned. She had bought a wedding dress. How can this happen?" He said it like it was a speech, like he had been thinking about it for a long time. Maybe he had had a sense that Tammy Lee was dead for a while.

"I'm sorry for your loss."

He turned on her. "That's what they all say. Sorry for your loss. What a stupid thing. Sorry that your wife-to-be died. That you'll never see her again. That you'll never get to marry her. We had the wedding band and everything."

"Do you have any idea who could have done this?"

"Well, I think you should be looking right in your own department. Andrew Stickler had every reason to kill her."

Amy stepped back. "Why would Andrew want to kill her?"

"He wanted to get her away from me. They broke up when he went into the service and Tammy Lee told me that he's been bugging her lately, wanting to see her."

"But why would he kill her?"

"Because she was with me, because she was going to marry me and he couldn't have her." Terry grabbed the sides of the table as his voice rose.

"I'll check into that. Anyone else?"

"Oh, geez." He wiped at his face. "Tammy Lee didn't always hang around with the best people. And I was gone a lot, on the railroad. She promised me she was being good, you know, not doing much drugs, not going to the bars, but she liked to have a good time, what can I say."

"What people? What bars?"

"Oh, you know, around. Some in Durand, she'd go up to Menomonie or even Eau Claire sometimes. I don't know. I didn't keep track. When she was with me, we'd stay close to home, but I know she could wander."

"Can you give me any names?"

As he told her a couple of men's names, Amy wrote them down. But her mind was still on the possibility of Andrew having something to do with this. She liked him and he was one of them now, a cop. It made her uncomfortable to think about checking up on him.

"Thanks," Amy said. "And where were you Friday night?"

"Just getting off the road. Got in about nine or ten that night. Went right to sleep. After my shift I'm beat. Tried to call Tammy Lee, but didn't get her. Figured I'd see her in the morning."

"Yeah," Amy said.

He sat down on the bench by the table and put his head in his hands. "When she knew I was home she'd often come pounding on my door in the morning, bringing me a doughnut or something. She could be so sweet."

"If you think of anything, give me a call."

At first Terry appeared to have hardly heard her, then he lifted his head and asked questions she couldn't answer. "What are they going to do with the bones? How will they bury her if that's all that's left?"

❧

The phone rang on his bedside table and Andrew grabbed it, still half asleep. "Yeah, who is it?"

"I know it's late."

Andrew sat up in bed. Her voice woke him up. He hadn't quite fallen asleep yet and had been thinking about her.

"Where are you?" he asked Meg.

"I'm outside my house, standing at the end of the driveway. It's where we get the best reception for my cell phone."

"You should be in bed and asleep. What're you doing up so late? You shouldn't be calling me."

"I know my mom talked to you, and I know she doesn't want us to see each other for a while, but I had to talk to you myself. Just to make sure this is what we want to do." Meg paused, then asked, "Can she order you not to see me?"

"Not really. But I think she's right. Until this death is cleared up, it would be for the best."

Meg didn't say anything.

"Are you still there?" he asked.

"Just like that. You're going to give in."

"It won't be forever."

"But I'm leaving in a couple of months."

"I know."

She sighed. "Can't we just get together to talk it over? I'd like to feel like it's our decision, not just something we're doing for my mom and your boss."

He knew it wasn't wise, but hearing her voice made him want to touch her again. "Okay. When and where?"

"How about the old wayside rest near Double J? You know, the one they shut down a few years ago. We could park there and no one would see us."

"When?"

"I've got to work tonight, but how about tomorrow night. Say, seven?" Meg suggested.

"Okay. I'll see you then." He knew he sounded reluctant.

"Is this really okay, or don't you want to see me?" Meg asked.

Andrew gave a sharp laugh. "You gotta understand. I'm just out of the service. I'm used to obeying orders."

CHAPTER 11

When Amy called the railroad company, she got some hoarse man at the other end shouting at her. "What? Just wait a minute while I close the door. What'd ya say?"

"I'm calling about Terry Whitman?"

"Yeah, what about him? He in trouble again?"

Amy was surprised by his question and not sure how to answer it, so for the moment she ignored it. "I'm calling from the Pepin County Sheriff's Department, and I'm checking on Mr. Whitman's work schedule."

"Oh, give me a sec. I got to dig to find it. He's got a few days off, then he starts back to work in three days."

"What about last week? When did he come off his shift?"

"Yeah, he worked until late on Friday."

"How late?"

"Depends on when we pulled in. I'd say it was probably around eight. I think we were pretty on schedule that night."

"Don't suppose you know where he went?"

"Ma'am, I don't know and don't care. Long as he's here when he's supposed to be."

"Right."

"But I do know that a lot of the guys go over to the Fourth Base after their shift is over. It's kinda a hangout for the railroad crew. Wouldn't surprise me if he stopped off there."

"Thanks, you've been a lot of help."

"What's he done this time?"

"He's been in trouble with the law before?" Amy asked.

"Oh, he gets in fights, nothing serious. Just got a temper. Not on the job, though. If he did it while he worked, he'd get the can. I heard he's getting married. Maybe that'll calm him down."

"Well, that's why I'm calling. His fiancée was killed."

"Lord, I'm sorry. Terry thought the world of her. He even showed her picture to a few of us. Seemed pretty happy about the whole deal. That's going to hit him hard. I'll pass the news around."

"If you talk to anyone who was with him Friday night, let me know."

"Sure will do. Terrible thing, terrible."

❧

Claire always liked the drive down to Rochester, the steep rise on the Minnesota side of the Mississippi up and out of the river valley to the rolling farmland. The bluffs on the west side were often in shadow, so as she drove up the road, she felt like she was lifting out into sunlight. Even just to get away from the department for a few hours felt good.

Earlier that day, Sheriff Talbert's wife had told her that the surgeons at Mayo had confirmed that putting in stents would not be enough to fix the sheriff's ailing heart, and they were going to do the quadruple bypass surgery the next day. Claire felt like she needed to see him before he was incapacitated for a week or so. Check in with him about a couple of things pending, but also talk to him about Andrew Stickler and what had happened to Tammy Lee.

She didn't want to have this conversation over the phone. His wife had assured her that he was in good enough shape to have a visit.

And if she would admit it to herself, Claire wanted to see the sheriff. He was a touchstone for her, a solid person she had come to rely on and she was feeling unsure of her ability to take his place, even for a month or so.

As she drove up over the bluff line and into the sun, she realized with a start that what she wanted was his blessing.

Another forty minutes and she drove into Rochester. She didn't go there too often and was always surprised by how completely the Mayo Clinic dominated the town—one posh neighborhood was even called Surgeon's Hill. Because of the squad car she could park wherever she pleased, but she did find a place in a lot not too far from the main hospital.

The other thing she learned about the Mayo Clinic as she entered the lobby, which was a pleasant surprise, was how much money and wall space they donated to artwork. Walking down the halls was like walking into a gallery. In one of the children's wings, she had seen an amazing ABC animal hooked rug that had really inspired her. Maybe when she retired she'd take up rug hooking.

When she came to his room, the TV was on but the sheriff was sleeping, and his wife was knitting something out of bright red yarn. Probably something for Christmas. Ella motioned her in.

Claire couldn't believe how pasty white the sheriff looked, worse than the last time she had seen him. "Don't wake him."

"He needs to get up anyway. Lunch will be here in a few minutes, and he won't want to miss that. Although they've got him on a low-cholesterol diet and he's not very happy about it."

"Don't imagine."

"I told him those eggs for breakfast every morning would catch up with him." Ella reached over, grabbed his foot through the light blanket, and wiggled it.

"Huh?" The sheriff startled awake.

"Calm down. Claire's here to see you. Isn't that nice?"

"Just doing her job," he said, although Claire could tell he was pleased. He turned to her, his eyes watery. "How's it going?"

"Well, I do need your help."

He pushed himself up in bed and wiped at his face. "With what? You're in charge."

"I know, but you still know the territory a lot better than I do." Claire told him about the bones that had been found in the Burning Boat, Tammy Lee Johansen gone missing, then the discovery that they were one and the same.

"Never heard of such a thing," he said.

"Well, it might have gone unnoticed if the kids hadn't put pots in the boat for a school project."

"So you think he just wanted to get rid of the body. Why not throw her in the river?"

"Remember a few years ago, the body that was floating by Point No Point? I think people now know that isn't a foolproof way."

"Well, dig a frickin' hole, then. Why go to the trouble of putting her in the boat?"

"I'm hoping to find out. She was engaged to be married to Terry Whitman, works for the railroad. You heard of him?"

"Yeah, he's not from the area. We've heard he's been in a fight or two, but no one's pressed charges. But let's say it's established that he has a temper."

"Well, the other suspect at the moment unfortunately is our own Deputy Andrew Stickler."

"What? How's he messed up in this?"

"I guess he was going out with Tammy Lee before he joined the service." Claire had decided that she didn't need to mention who Andrew had been dating most recently.

"I don't know this Tammy Lee, but if she was dating Terry, then Andrew just doesn't seem her type."

"Who knows. They were just out of high school. I'm concerned about how to handle it with Andrew. Should I ask him to take a leave?"

"One thing at a time, Claire. He have an alibi for time of death?"

"Well, the time of death is rather broad. We know Tammy was alive early on Friday and the boat was burned on Saturday evening. However, there was a lot of activity in the park all afternoon—so she was probably killed either Friday night or early Saturday morning."

"This Whitman guy? Where was he?"

"He got off work around eight Friday night. He claims he went home and hit the hay. Would make sense, since he was working an eight-day shift, but maybe Tammy Lee was waiting for him at his house."

"What about Andrew?"

"You know he's still staying with his folks. He says that he watched some TV with them and then they all went off to bed. So who knows. He could have snuck out after that. There has been some contact between Andrew and Tammy Lee since he's come back. I'm not sure how much or what it means."

"Yeah." The sheriff rubbed his jawline, which was rough with stubble.

"When you hired him, did you get his service record?"

"Sure. I mean, Andrew's a good guy. He even got some sort of medal for courage in the line of duty. Something bad went down when he was fighting over there and a couple guys got killed, but he saved a guy's life. I didn't read it all—but it's in the report they sent us."

Claire hadn't known that, and she took it in. Andrew did seem like a good guy. Maybe she had been too hard on him.

"I'd keep looking at Terry if I were you," he said.

"Oh, I intend to, sir, but I don't want to overlook anything."

"Not worried about you doing that, Claire. Sounds like you've got things under control."

"Thanks," she said as a nurse wheeled in a tray: broth in a bowl, a fruit cup, and skim milk. "I don't think I'll be staying for lunch."

"Go eat a hamburger for me," the sheriff said.

"Good luck, sir, with your surgery."

He waved his hand at her. "They're going to fix me up just fine."

❦

Doug remembered the smell of the old barn, fermenting hay, old wood, and a tang of rusting metal. When he was a kid it had been a working barn, used for the cows and for his granddad's workshop. Now the roof was starting to sag and the sides were weathered almost silver-gray where the paint had worn off. He wondered how much longer it would last.

Maybe longer than him.

He sat down on a bale of hay and thought about how he would do this thing he planned on doing. He had been working on the plan for so long—it's what kept him going—and now it was going to happen and then where would he be?

He shook himself, like a horse shakes the flies from its neck. Thoughts were like pesky insects, biting in places you couldn't reach. Put one foot in front of the other, like his granddad used to say. And look where it got him. Killed one day when the tractor backed up over him. Grandma just shook her head, said she thought he loved the tractor as much he loved anything. Now look what happened, she said.

Doug was only six and they didn't let him go to the funeral. He had walked around the farm, putting one foot in front of the other, while the tractor sat out by the end of the driveway with a For Sale sign hanging on the radiator.

After that, Grandma sold off pieces of the farm when she needed money. Now all she had left was the house and the falling-down barn.

When Doug had joined the service, he had taken out an insurance policy in his grandmother's name. He figured it was the least he could do. No one else was watching out for her.

He walked over to the tool chest that Granddad had built into the side of the barn. Not much of a carpenter; it was a rather shabby affair with a few assorted tools left in it. But there was a secret compartment built behind it that he had seen Granddad put the gun in one day, nearly twenty years ago. He was counting on it still being there.

Pulling out the board, he saw that something was in there, wrapped up in an old pillowcase. When he lifted the object out of its hiding place, it was heavy and hard, cold from years of neglect.

Turning back the pillowcase, he saw the barrel of the old gun. It was smaller than he remembered it. When he was a kid, the gun had looked huge and so powerful. He almost laughed to look at it now. Puny.

When he thought of what he had been shooting with in Afghanistan, this was like a slingshot. He closed the chest, sat on the top of it, and looked the gun over. Not big, but a solid piece of work. It needed to be cleaned up and oiled, but it would do the trick.

When he walked into the kitchen with the gun in his hands, Grandma had looked at the gun and then him and said, "What you fixing to shoot?"

He laid it on the table. "Pheasant. You want to fix me up some pheasant?"

"Might could do."

"We'll have us a feast tonight."

CHAPTER 12

Claire didn't know the Sticklers very well. She had met them once or twice, but they were pretty quiet people, farmers, and didn't get in any trouble. She hated to bother them about Andrew, but it had to be done.

She could have sent Amy—after all, Claire was the sheriff now and should be sticking around the department more than she was—but she felt like this was her call. She wanted this interview to be handled just right. Andrew wasn't telling her everything, and she needed to know what he was keeping from her.

The farmhouse was set back a good distance from the road, with a stand of pine trees growing on the north side of the house, a solid windbreak. The house was an old four-square with a front porch, probably built at the turn of the last century, a big front door right in the middle of it.

But as with most houses, the door that was used the most was around the back and led into the kitchen. Claire parked so that she wasn't blocking the driveway and knocked on the back door. No answer, but there was a truck and a Buick LeSabre parked next to each other. Someone should be home.

Claire knocked again, tried the door and found it open. She was just about to walk in when Mrs. Stickler came to the door. Although her hair was streaked with gray, she moved like a younger woman, full of energy. She was wearing jeans and a sweatshirt that had a horse on it, and had a laundry basket propped on her hip. "Sorry. I was in the basement, doing the wash." Her face blanched. "Andrew okay?"

"Yes, he's fine. Mind if I come in?"

Mrs. Stickler scooted back out of the way and showed Claire to a chair at the kitchen table. "We're so glad to have him back, and now with this good job and everything . . . well, I just can't tell you."

Claire could imagine. Just thinking of Meg going away to college was turning her upside down, but to send your child around the world to fight in a war where he might get killed? Too much to ask.

"And we're glad to have him. He's a great addition to the force," Claire said, and was surprised how rote she sounded. "But I'm going to have ask you a few questions about his whereabouts the other night."

"What night?" Mrs. Stickler sank into a chair opposite Claire.

"Friday night."

"Oh, we were all here. Watching some TV. Clarence and I try to make it to the news. Doesn't always happen, but then we went to bed."

"Andrew too?"

"Well, I suppose. He stayed on in the living room. Lets us use the bathroom first, you know. I thought I heard him come upstairs. Hard to be sure. Some nights I just go out like a light. But where would he go?"

"Does he ever just go out for a drink?"

"Not much. Most of his old friends aren't around anymore. Plus, he doesn't like to drink if he's gotta work the next day. He's real conscientious that way."

"You know Tammy Lee Johansen, Mrs. Stickler?"

"Sure I know her. Since she was a little girl. Andrew and she were real close for a while, but it was hard when he went off. I think they stayed in touch. I'm not quite sure what happened there."

"Well, I'm sorry to tell you, but Tammy died on Friday night."

"Oh no." Mrs. Stickler brought her hands up to her mouth. "Car accident? She drinks a lot, I know."

"No, unfortunately someone hit her and killed her."

Mrs. Stickler stood up as if she'd been shot. "Not Andrew," she said in a wail. "Never would he do that."

"I'm not saying he did. I'm just checking on things. According to Tammy Lee's sister, they'd seen each other."

"Yes, that's right. I think Andrew ran into her at a bar, and Tammy did call here once or twice recently, asking for Andrew. I didn't think too much of it. I heard she's engaged to be married to some railroad guy."

"Do you know if Andrew and she got together?"

"Not that I know of—but I don't keep track of Andrew's goings-on. It's not easy on him, living back at home at his age, but he's saving up to buy a house. I told him he can come and go as he pleases, just to be quiet if it's too late."

Just then Mr. Stickler walked in, a solid man wearing a barn coat and a John Deere hat. "Andrew here?"

Claire stood up and shook his hand. "No, I'm Claire Watkins." Then she made herself say it: "Acting sheriff."

"That so?" He took off his hat and she saw the white line across his forehead: farmer's tan. "What can we do for you?"

"She was just asking about Andrew. That poor Tammy Lee was killed," Mrs. Stickler broke in. "I told her Andrew was home with us on Friday night."

Mr. Stickler nodded slowly. "That's right. We all went to bed after the news. Same as usual."

"He couldn't have gone out again?" Claire asked.

"Might have, but I doubt it. I don't sleep that sound anymore. But some nights he don't sleep so well either. He gets up and goes for a walk. It's been hard on him, being back here, readjusting."

"Has he seen Tammy Lee, as far as you know?"

"Don't really know. But if he did, it was just for old times' sake. He had just starting going out with some new girl—seemed to be quite interested in her. Guess she's smart as a whip. Didn't say who she was."

Claire felt a jolt as she realized who they were talking about. She thanked them and walked toward the door.

Mrs. Stickler said, "Sorry to hear about Tammy Lee. She wasn't a bad girl—just had a lot of gumption. She would have settled down, I'm sure."

ᐳᐸ

Meg sat on the edge of her bed with the phone in her hand. She was going to call Andrew and tell him she wanted to see him tonight. Even though she knew they shouldn't meet.

She put the phone down and wiped tears away. It felt like someone else was being taken away from her before she even had a chance to know him. Like her dad. She picked up the last picture she had of her father before he was killed.

In it, Dad and she stood happily together, just back from trick or treating. She had been a ballerina. Looking back, she saw that it had been a ridiculous choice, but she had been going through a pink phase, a girly phase. Her mom had been too busy to come up with much of a costume, so her dad had run out at the last minute, when all the costumes were gone, and bought three pink slips that she wore one on top of the other. He had made her a tiara out of tin foil. She'd thought she looked beautiful.

Her mom had come through in the hairdo and make-up department, pulling her dark hair back in a tight bun that gave her a headache and putting on pink lipstick.

In the picture her tall dad was holding her hand: a bedraggled ballerina, slips drooping, a puffy purple jacket over her outfit, and a crown that sat sideways on her head.

But she looked so happy.

She had a full bag of candy and for the last few houses her dad had let her run up all by herself, as if she was old enough to be on her own, and ring the doorbell and yell, "Trick or treat!"

Her dad had pretended he could hardly carry her bag of candy, it was so full.

After he had died, Meg let the bag of candy sit in its hiding place under her bed until, months later, her mom made her throw all the dried-up, rotten candy away.

Meg put the picture back on her bedside table, then picked up the phone and dialed Andrew's cell number. He answered after three rings. "Stickler."

"Watkins. I guess I should say Meg." Hearing his voice, she knew how much she wanted to see him again.

"Hey." His voice lit up. "We still on for tonight?"

"Just to talk." Meg said. "I'd like to meet you tonight—just to say goodbye for a while."

There was a long silence, then he said in a low voice, "Whatever."

"Where's Meg?" Claire asked when just she and Rich sat down for dinner.

"She went out about an hour ago. Didn't say where she was going, but said she wouldn't be home for dinner," he said as he put a platter of pork chops on the table. Steaming mashed potatoes and a bowl of corn the color of butter sat next to it.

"I asked Andrew Stickler not to see her for a while."

"That's fine," Rich said as he took a pork chop.

"Is it?" She lifted her head up and searched his face. He always felt more levelheaded than she did. He didn't seem to worry quite as much.

"Yes, he's under your command, he's involved somewhat in this case, you're just taking prudent precautions."

That made Claire smile. "I like that phrase: 'prudent precautions.' That does describe it, but I feel like I'm not trusting my daughter to make her own decisions."

"You get to be wrong once in a while, Claire."

"So you think it's wrong?"

"No, I just don't think you need to worry about it so much. Your daughter is near perfect. You've done a great job raising her. She'll figure it out, even if it means breaking the rules sometimes."

"I know you're right. I know it. But this case has got me all jittery."

"Eat your supper. That will make you feel better."

"Nothing like a pork chop to calm a person down," she said as she grabbed a chop and piled mashed potatoes and corn on her plate.

They ate in silence. But Claire couldn't stop thinking about the case. It was digging into her in a horridly uncomfortable way. Was she getting tired? Was it the way the murder had been done— the burned bones? Was it her age?

Or was it that she was now the sheriff—whatever that meant—and she was more in charge than ever, completely responsible?

She hated that one of her own men was somewhat involved with this murder—if she was honest, even in spite of Andrew's alibi that mainly checked out—he was still a suspect.

Then there was Meg.

That was it—her daughter was at the center of it all.

Claire would do anything not to have her hurt.

Rich reached over and touched her hand. "What's going on in that mind of yours?"

"Oh, you know the usual. Why would anyone kill Tammy Lee Johansen? Why do we kill each other?"

Rich rubbed her hand, but he gave her no answer.

CHAPTER 13

Meg had walked down to the wayside rest from Rich's house. It wasn't that far, maybe about a mile; however, it was colder out than she'd thought, and she wished she had worn gloves. She stood by the edge of the parking lot and rubbed her hands, waiting to see the Jeep's lights turn off the road.

Then, just to look like she wasn't waiting so hard, she turned herself around and stared at the lake. The color of the water was turning. As the weather got colder, it appeared to Meg that the lake turned sluggish gray as it thickened toward ice. Odd to think that she would be gone from this place soon. To live someplace in the city, without the huge presence of the river to always be beside her. From her bedroom window she could look out and see the lake.

Hearing tires on gravel, she spun around and saw Andrew's Jeep pull into the lot. He drove right up to her and stopped a few feet away. Almost in a single motion, he turned off the car and jumped out.

"You look cold," he said. "You want to get into the car?"

As much as Meg wanted to be in the warmth, she knew that being that close to him in an enclosed space would not be a good idea right now. She needed the answers to some questions before she would be comfortable with him. "No, I'm fine. Who knows how much longer it will be this warm."

"So we're talking about the weather now?" he asked as he walked up to her and put his hands on her shoulders.

Tears came to her eyes. She wiped at them.

"Hey, what's the matter?" he said. "This isn't going to last long."

"No, it's not this." She waved her arm. "I've been thinking about my dad."

"You mean your real dad?" he asked. She had told him that her father had been killed in the Twin Cities when she was young.

"Yeah, you know they always say it's the death that's so hard. I know for me, because it was so dramatic, getting run down by a car, that's often what everyone else has reacted to. But it wasn't the awfulness of his death that has haunted me. It's the hole, the missing, the gone forever part of it. Do you know what I mean?"

He nodded, and then as if sensing she needed a word, said, "Completely."

"That goneness never ends. Birthdays, Christmas, and he's not there."

"I'm sorry, Meg."

"Well, I don't want you to go away, just when I met you."

"I won't."

She tucked her head and lowered her voice. "I wish you could have met him, that he could have met you."

"But isn't Rich like your dad now?" he asked.

Meg lifted her head quickly. "Absolutely. And he's the best. Don't get me wrong. But I come from my dad. Mom says I have his weird sense of humor, even his laugh."

She was forced to look into his eyes. They were smiling at her.

"That's where you get that deep laugh." Then he touched her face and said, "It's going to be fine. We'll figure out what happened to Tammy Lee, and then we'll be able to see each other again."

"My mom talked to you."

"Yup, the sheriff herself."

"I heard you went out with her—that girl that got killed."

He nodded. "I did. When I was a kid. Before I joined the service. Feels like another century. Weren't a lot of choices around this area. Besides, I had no idea you even existed."

"Well, no, because when you were twenty, I was twelve."

"Bet you were cute then."

"Rather awkward. Braces, wild hair, pimples. No, twelve wasn't one of my better ages."

He leaned forward and kissed her on the nose. "Cute."

While she wanted to lean into him, feel the comfort of his jacket, his arms, she stepped back slightly and asked, "Have you seen her since you've been back from Afghanistan?"

"Hey, I don't mind getting the third degree from your mom. It's her job. But what's with you?"

"I can't help it. I want to know what's going on."

"I did see her a time or two, but just because we ran into each other. It was okay. You know she was engaged to be married. She wanted to get together, but I told her I was busy. Didn't have any need to see her."

"Who broke it off between you?"

He looked down at the ground. "I did. I'm not proud of it, but I had to. I just felt so far away from everything when I was in Afghanistan. I couldn't handle even thinking about home. So I wrote her an e-mail. I know it's the coward's way, but I didn't get the feeling it broke her heart. She agreed immediately. I think she was tired of waiting for me. Tammy liked to have a good time in all ways."

"Okay, too much information."

"Look, Meg. She was my first girlfriend. We had fun together. But that's all. I'm not saying that what you and I have is more.

Who knows. We just met. But already I feel like we have more in common than Tammy and I ever did."

"Oh," Meg said. His words were making her feel better, but she wanted to get even warmer. "Maybe we could get into the car. It is rather cold out here."

⁊

When the phone rang, Claire was just brushing her teeth. She spit out the toothpaste and ran for the phone, as Rich was already asleep in bed. Meg hadn't come home yet. She was probably calling to tell them where she was. Not that Claire was worried.

"Hello?" she said.

"Yeah, is this the deputy?" a gruff man's voice asked.

"Yes, this is Claire Watkins." She didn't recognize the voice and didn't feel like explaining that she was actually the sheriff for the time being.

"Yeah, well, I heard you called. I camp down to the park nearly every weekend. My name's Gib Swenson. Live up Double S a ways."

"Oh, yes?"

"Well, I just heard about the bones that were found in the fire. You know, the big boat. That was something, that fire. We had a ringside seat, the wife and me, right by our RV."

"Do you know something about the bones?" Claire asked.

"Not for sure, but we set up our RV the night before the big burn. We came down after work, so it was getting kinda late. I'd say it was after nine o'clock. Anyway, we got it all set and we were getting ready for bed. I had a snack, some cereal, I often do that. Sitting in the front part of the RV at the window, just looking out at the lake, thinking, you know."

Mary Logue

Claire sighed. He was taking his time, but she didn't want to rush him. She listened carefully.

"Then I thought I saw a movement over by the boat. Didn't think too much of it, because they'd been working on that thing pretty much night and day for the last couple weeks. But still, it seemed kinda strange because I could see someone moving, but I couldn't see no lights on."

"How could you see anything?"

"Well, there's the lights in the park, they let me see a little, although they're not very close to the boat. The moon was out, too—not full, but gave off some light. And this was the other thing—it looked like he was carrying something. Again, I didn't think much of it, because they were always putting more stuff on the boat to make sure it would burn. But the way he was carrying it, slung over his back, seemed odd."

"Now, you're saying 'he.' Do you think it was a man?"

"Now that you mention it, I guess I just assumed it was a man. Kind of a big guy, had to be strong to be carrying that load. The way he moved. Yeah, I'm pretty sure it was a man."

"Then what happened?"

"Well, he disappeared. Couldn't see him anymore. I washed out my dish—the wife doesn't like me to leave it dirty in the sink—and went back to the window. The man stepped away from the boat and he wasn't carrying anything anymore. Then he walked out to the road right there and got into a vehicle and drove away."

"What kind of vehicle?"

"Some kind of car, couldn't see it that good, muffler going a bit. Do you think that was the guy who done it? Who killed that girl?"

"Could be. What time did you say this was?"

"Well, I figure it was close to eleven. I watched the news and got ready for bed before I ate the cereal. Yeah, pretty close to eleven."

"Could you come down to the department tomorrow so we could get a statement from you, Mr. Swenson? Anything you can remember would be a help."

"Sure. I've got chores in the morning, but I could come in after that." He didn't say anything for a moment. Then he asked, "Do you think if I would have gone out there I could have saved her?"

"Probably not. Plus you could have gotten hurt yourself."

"If I would have known . . . ." He trailed off.

"You've helped us with this information. Thanks for calling."

"When I heard about the bones, I wondered. Terrible thing."

❧

Doug lay on his back in the twin bed in his grandmother's spare room, and tried not to go to sleep. His nightmares were getting worse. Always he was back in Afghanistan, in those craggy hills, climbing through the rocks and bushes, trying to stay alive, trying to get away from whatever was following him.

He couldn't stand the dreams anymore. He had to stop them. And he knew what he had to do.

He was all ready. Tomorrow or the next day he would carry out his mission. Call Andrew and set it up. Time to get this baby off his back. He almost didn't care what would happen to him afterward. He had taken a vow, and he would stick to it.

Closing his eyes, he tried to stay alert. He could feel them all around him, creeping up. There was no way he could get out of the hole he was in.

He jerked his eyes open. The light shining down the hallway was like a star in the sky, showing him he was in his grandmother's house. He could hear her gentle snore in the next room.

He reached down and felt the stock of the gun that was lying beside the bed. The cold metal reassured him. He had what he needed.

He closed his eyes again. This time he was walking forward, not skulking in the weeds. He was taking action. He was carrying out his last duty. It would be enough.

Sleep poured over him like enemy waves, swamping him in the dark.

CHAPTER 14

"Let's go into the sheriff's office," Claire suggested as she tapped Amy on the shoulder.

"You finally going to move in there?" Amy asked, getting up and following her down the hallway.

"Not yet. Hopefully not ever. I'm counting on the sheriff coming back. Just feels too strange to take over his office, plus I like being out on the floor. But I want to talk about Tammy Lee Johansen—where we're at, and figure out what to do next. You got all the information from Mr. Swenson?"

As they settled into the sheriff's office, Claire forced herself to go around the desk and sit down in his chair. The office chair was too big for her and not in good shape. It held the imprint of the sheriff's large body. Probably just right for him. She, however, felt like Goldilocks.

Claire perched on the edge of the big chair and said, "What more did you get from him? Seemed like a garrulous old guy."

"I doubt if it's anything you haven't heard, but I've been checking with more of the campers. So far he's the only one who noticed the car that came that night. I'm thinking we should be searching Terry Whitman's car."

"Yes, I'd like you to bring in Terry Whitman's car and go over it thoroughly. And have a look at Andrew's, too. Andrew's regular vehicle is that brand new Jeep. Doubt it has a muffler problem, but still might be worth looking at."

"We know there's going to be Tammy Lee's fingerprints in Terry's car." Amy brought out a piece of paper from her file and handed it to Claire. "Also, we lucked out with her. She shoplifted something in tenth grade, so we've got her fingerprints on file. But who knows what else we might find in there."

"Do you want me to tell Andrew that we want to search his car, or are you up for it?" Claire asked.

Amy wrinkled her nose. "I'd rather not. I've barely got seniority over him. It'd be better coming from you."

"Not a problem. I'll catch him as soon as he gets in and ask him if we can go over the vehicle. Why don't you give it a once over, and if you find anything that makes you think we should inspect it more carefully, we'll call the lab."

"Sure." Amy looked down at her notes, then looked up and said, "I just have to say this. I can't believe Andrew had anything to do with Tammy's death. I'm not saying he wouldn't or couldn't kill someone. I just don't think he'd put her body in the boat. I think it's too weird for him."

Claire didn't say anything. Let Amy have her say.

"He's just not that kind of guy. Plus, Andrew doesn't need to force himself on a woman. He's cute and well behaved."

"So are many sociopaths," Claire couldn't help pointing out.

"But he's not like that."

"War does hard things to men."

Amy shook her head. "I guess. I just have a hard time believing Andrew would do something like that. It's too creepy."

"Yeah, there is a large creep factor in it. Makes me wonder if we're looking at someone who's done this before."

"Like a serial killer?" Amy's voice rose.

"Maybe not killed before, but done something with fires. I think you're right, putting her in the boat to be burned. Worth checking out. Ask around about Terry. He doesn't have a record, but see if there's ever been any trouble when he's been around, any arson." Claire let out a sigh. "At least I don't need to check on Andrew. That stuff would have come out when we were hiring him."

❧

"Why didn't you go to Vietnam?" Meg asked Rich as they sat at the kitchen table, cracking black walnuts open and digging out the meat.

There were hundreds of black walnut trees on their property, and every fall Meg and Rich would crack open enough of them to make a cake or two. The nuts were not easy to shell, and to get even a cup of the walnuts took a lot of work. Not to mention husking them and curing them and soaking them. But when Rich made his black walnut cake with buttercream icing, Meg thought it was all worth it.

"Vietnam?" He lifted out a perfect nugget of a nut to show her. "I was a little bit too young. Plus I worked on a farm. We get special dispensation sometimes."

"Would you have gone if they had drafted you?"

Rich slammed a hammer into a nut, and it shattered. "I don't know. I doubt it. Don't really believe in all that stuff."

"What stuff?"

"Killing, fighting."

"So you don't believe in war?"

"Oh, I guess I'd say it might be a necessary evil, but not one I'd like to participate in. Also, sending all the young men off to fight when they don't even know they could be killed, when they haven't even lived, some of them haven't had a drink, haven't been laid."

"Rich." Meg was surprised by how blunt he was being.

"You asked me. If we drafted the old men, like my age, I doubt there'd be many wars. I for one wouldn't go."

"Well, I think war is just plain evil."

He looked up at her, the hammer raised to strike another nut. "Good for you, Megster."

"Do you think Mom is right—not wanting me to see Andrew?"

"Oh, you'd like me to get in the middle of that?" He slammed the hammer down and the nut broke in two perfect halves.

"You've got a good aim," Meg laughed. "I guess it's probably been hard on you, not taking sides."

"Sometimes," Rich said. "But mainly I'm glad it's not my decision."

"What do you think about me seeing Andrew?"

"To tell you the truth, I'd leave it up to you, but I have to say your mom doesn't ask much of you—and this is her business. She knows more than me when it comes to the ways of the world. I'm just a lowly pheasant farmer."

"Which rhymes with peasant farmer, or pleasant farmer."

"You got it."

"Let me have the hammer. You're having all the fun."

He handed the hammer to Meg. "You need to take out a little of that aggression, too, I guess."

"Yes, this is the last time Mom can tell me what to do." To punctuate that statement, she slammed the hammer down on a walnut. Unfortunately, she hit it too hard and the whole thing flew into bits.

"Somehow, I don't think you're listening to her," Rich said, chipping away carefully at a nut.

"Whatever gives you that idea?"

"You seem happier than I think you would be if you really weren't seeing Andrew." He winked at her.

Meg brought the hammer down with a little more care. "Pheasant farmer and soothsayer."

☙

Andrew walked in right on time from his shift. Claire knew because she was waiting for him. She wondered how he would react to her request. He could demand a search warrant, but she doubted he would do that. Just wouldn't be very smart.

She walked up to him as he was coming around the counter. "How's it going?"

He looked at her and tried a half smile. "Not bad."

"Hey, Andrew, I'm sorry to say this, but we're going to have to search your car. Do I have your permission?"

He stood still and his gaze turned inward, thinking. Without much of a pause, he nodded. "I guess. It's not here. I drove the squad car home last night. You want me to go and get it?"

"No, I'll send Amy out for it. You can drive her out there. Just stay away from the vehicle."

His eyes hardened. "I know how to handle this. Don't worry."

He stalked off and went to get Amy.

When Claire got back to her desk, the phone rang. She was glad to have something else to think about. She couldn't help feeling bad about Andrew. No matter how much she didn't want him seeing her daughter, he still seemed like a good guy to her.

A shattered woman's voice said, "This is Mrs. Johansen. Can I speak to that woman, Watkins whatever her name is?"

"Speaking," Claire said. "How can I help you, Mrs. Johansen?"

"Well, they delivered the bones, like you said they would. But it's just bones." The woman started crying.

"I'm so sorry. This must be so hard."

"Yes, but you see, there's the ring."

"What ring?"

"Her engagement ring. She told me it was worth a thousand dollars, a real diamond and all. But I can't find no ring in with the bones."

"I don't think a ring was found."

"But it wouldn't have melted. It must be there someplace."

"I was with the forensic bone guy, and he made a completely thorough search of the burn site."

"Well, a ring is heavier. Maybe it went deeper than he looked."

"That's a possibility."

"Maybe I'll go down and look for it."

"No, I don't think that's a good idea. I'll check into it and get back to you later today."

"That ring is mine," the woman said fiercely.

Claire wasn't going to argue with her, but she wasn't sure what the law was on that. It might actually belong to Terry Whitman; after all, he gave it to Tammy Lee as a promise of marriage.

"We'll find it," Claire assured her, then asked, "How're you doing with everything, Mrs. Johansen?"

The woman broke into sobs, then when she quieted, she said, "My daughter's dead and all I've got is a bag of bones and ash. I don't know what to do. I just don't know what to do."

CHAPTER 15

"I'm just double-checking with you, Dr. Pinkers. Did you find a ring when you searched the burn site?" Claire stood by her desk, ready to hit the road if she got the answer she was afraid she would get from the forensic anthropologist.

"I found a couple of nails, but no ring." He sighed, then continued, "I would have told you if I had. I didn't really have to dig down very far to extract the bones. They were all lying in order and I just carefully picked them up. Since they hadn't been messed with and none of them were missing, I didn't look any further." He cleared his throat, then continued, "If you're looking for a ring in that mess, I'd use a metal detector."

"I know we have one somewhere. That's a good thought."

"You know," the doctor drew the phrase out, "whoever did this might have taken off the ring before putting her there."

"Yes, I've thought of that too."

"Nasty business."

"No doubt. But I'm going to try to find it."

"There's a lot of metal in those old pallets, so you're going to find nails and staples galore."

As Claire drove down to Fort St. Antoine with the metal detector in the back seat, she felt like she was on a hopeless mission. She also knew she should have sent someone else to do this search, but she had to get out of the office. She wasn't used to being under fluorescent lights all day long.

The day was warm for early October, and she rolled a window down to feel the air. If they didn't make a significant step forward on this case today, she was calling in the crime lab from Madison for help. She had been resisting because somehow she felt like the big guns would just trample what little evidence there was and not understand how people in this small county passed on information.

Just like the way she had been fifteen years ago, coming down from Minneapolis and thinking she knew it all. Rich had gently showed her she didn't. Her fellow deputies had not been quite so gentle. It had been painful, but it worked, and she had adjusted her skills to the ways of the country.

When she drove into the park, she saw two trailers were still parked near the beach. Odd for trailers to be in the park so late in the year, but the weather was holding. The one closest to the burn site she guessed was Mr. Swenson, and she needed to find out who the other one was, although Amy had probably already talked to them.

As she got out of the car, the wind picked up. The branches of the enormous cottonwoods creaked above her head and the wind whipped up whitecaps on the lake. But the air felt good to her, blowing some fatigue away.

Claire walked over and stood next to the charred remnants of the boat. She could vaguely make out the outlines of the body that had been lifted from the ashes. Yes, Dr. Pinkers had been very careful in removing the bones. He had disturbed little else. It made sense that something metal, being heavier than bone, might drop down farther into the remains of the fire.

She put on the metal detector headphones, turned on the machine, held out the search coil and swung it over the site. The detector crackled to life. She wondered if it really was going to be of much use. She was getting a lot of squeal. As Dr. Pinkers had predicted, the burn site was littered with metal, according to how much noise she was hearing from the machine.

Claire decided she'd have to notch it down to disregard objects that have a phase shift comparable to a pop-can tab or a small nail. Once she made this adjustment, she swung it slowly over the site again, getting much less squeal out of it.

In the middle of the site, she heard the pitch of the detector climb to a new height, almost like a fire siren. She swung the search coil over the area again and it squealed even louder. Time to take a look.

Claire turned off the detector, set it to the side, and knelt down by the burned boat. She pulled on latex gloves that went up to her elbows. She had also thought to bring a sifter with her. Digging in to the ash, she put it through the sifter, finding nails and bottle caps.

Going a little deeper, she felt something that had the shape of a tin can top, but seemed heavier. She grabbed it and pulled it out of the ash. Wiping it off, she saw that it was in the shape of a large coin.

Any trace of fingerprints that might have been on the object would have burned off in the fire, so she felt comfortable walking down to the water and dipping the metal piece into the lake. When it was washed off, she could make out some writing on it— for bravery in duty. A military medal. It looked recent.

She did not like this one bit. Why was everything pointing at Andrew?

છ

Andrew drove Amy out to his family's farm, which was about fifteen miles out of Durand. Amy felt uncomfortable sitting next to him—as if he was driving her to his own funeral or something. If they knew each other better, maybe they could joke about it, but she still felt like she didn't know Andrew that well. They hadn't worked together long and they weren't often partnered.

They were silent for most of the drive, but then she decided she better say something. "You know we have to do this. Just to check it off the list. Claire's real careful about stuff."

"I have no trouble with this search at all. I've got nothing to hide. So let's get it over with. I just want to do my job, and the sooner this is behind me the better. Tammy Lee's caused me enough trouble."

"I didn't know Tammy Lee hardly at all."

"Yeah, she was all right. For high school. But once I got out into the world, she didn't really want to know anything about what I was doing. She'd talk about friends from school, as if I cared. It was just such a disconnect from where I was—in a frigging war zone."

"I bet." Amy had always been curious about what he had done in Afghanistan. "How long were you over there?"

"Nearly four years."

"What was it like?"

He was quiet for a few moments. "Like it wasn't even on the same planet as here. I felt like we were on Mars or something. Astronauts in this weird land. The aliens not only didn't speak our language, but hated us, wouldn't look at us. Except for going out on forays we were pretty much confined to our little fortress. Life there was this odd mixture of boredom and fear."

They turned down the long driveway to the farm. Amy could see an old John Deere tractor parked next to the garage.

"That old tractor run?" she asked.

"Oh, yeah. Dad doesn't use it much any more, but he won't give up on it. It's a real workhorse."

They parked close to the house, and Andrew pointed to a Jeep. "It's open. Here's the keys."

Amy took them.

"I'm going in. Come in and have a cup of coffee when you're done." He turned to walk toward the house, then turned back. "Are you going to check for fingerprints?" he asked.

"Should I?" Amy hadn't planned on that unless she found something incriminating.

"Well, Tammy Lee was in my car once."

"Oh?" Amy waited.

"Yeah, I gave her a lift home from the bar a while ago. No big deal."

"You tell Claire?"

"I didn't think it was that important. Nothing happened. I mean, I just drove her home. You're not going to find anything else, but I thought you should know."

"Yeah, I'll come and get you when I'm done." His admission left Amy feeling even more uneasy than she had driving out. She felt like he wasn't telling them everything, and yet at the same time she couldn't believe he would kill Tammy Lee. When he talked about her, there just wasn't that much emotion in his voice. Hard to kill someone when you didn't care about them, one way or another.

Amy put on gloves and then opened the passenger side door. If Tammy Lee had been in the car, she might have left something around the seat. The vehicle was remarkably clean. A few gas receipts in the cup holder, car manual and a flashlight in the glove compartment, an orange peel under the passenger seat.

She went around and checked both the driver's side and the back seat. Again, not much. A windshield scraper for winter, a tire wrench tucked under the back seat, an empty bag of Fritos, a blanket folded on the back seat.

Amy carefully picked up the blanket. It was a Biederlack blanket, made out of some kind of polar fleece material. She unfolded the blanket, but nothing fell out. It smelled clean. Not a bad idea to keep something like that in a vehicle, especially in winter. She could see that Andrew liked to be prepared. If he hadn't been a Boy Scout, she'd be surprised.

As she was putting the blanket back on the seat, something caught her eye. A flash of silver by the front seat belt. She leaned forward and looked more closely. It looked like a pop can pull tab was stuck in the seat belt holder. She was able to wiggle her finger down into the holder and pull it out.

The object that she dropped into her hand was not a tab, but a ring with what looked like a tiny diamond. The ring size was so small that Amy didn't think it would even fit on her pinky finger. As she recalled, Tammy Lee was quite petite.

She put it in a plastic bag and walked slowly up to the farmhouse. When she stepped inside, Andrew and his mother were sitting at the kitchen table, drinking coffee. They both looked up and smiled at her. Then the smiles died.

"I found this," Amy said. She held out the bag so that Andrew could see it clearly. "It's a ring."

His mother drew in her breath. "Andrew," she said.

Andrew looked at the bag and then raised his eyes to Amy's. "I don't know anything about that ring. I've never seen it before in my life."

❧

Claire took the two of them back in the sheriff's office and closed the door. Since there were only three chairs in the room,

Claire put herself behind the desk and Andrew and Amy sat in the folding chairs facing her.

"Okay, what do you know about this ring?" Claire asked.

Andrew shook his head, his head lowered between his shoulders. "Not a blasted thing."

"But now you say that Tammy Lee was in your car?" Amy had told her that as she had handed her the bag with the ring.

"Yes, I would have said it before but I didn't think it was that important. It happened on Wednesday. You asked me about Friday. I had stopped in for a quick brew on my way home, she was at the bar, and I offered her a lift home. We're not on bad terms or anything. Hell, she's engaged. Or she was."

"Which is where this ring comes in. Her mother will be here shortly to identify it. So how did it get in your car? Could it be anyone else's?"

"I doubt it. I suppose it could be. I don't know anything about it."

"When you gave Tammy Lee a ride home was she wearing a ring?" Claire asked, feeling exasperated with him. He was a cop. He should notice things.

"I didn't notice, but I'd guess she was since she was engaged."

Calm down, she told herself, just ask him the questions you would ask any suspect. "What did the two of you talk about on that ride?"

Andrew started to say something, then stalled out. He looked up above Claire's head, out the window. The silence stretched on. Then he lowered his head and said, "She wanted to get back together with me again."

Claire leaned over the desk. "What do you mean?"

"She never wanted to break up. It was my idea. She said she didn't want to marry Terry and she wanted to get back with me."

"Did you want that?"

Andrew's eyes widened and then he snorted. "No way. Absolutely not. I was done with her years ago."

"How so?"

"Tammy Lee was fun for a while, but she wasn't someone I wanted to grow old with, much less grow up with. I felt that even more strongly when I came back home. We had nothing in common. She didn't want to know about Afghanistan. I don't even think she could find it on a map."

"But she broke up with you," Amy jumped in. "At least that's what her sister told me."

"Maybe that's what Tammy Lee told her, but that's not the way it went down. I e-mailed her and told her she should see other guys. I said that we should call it quits while I was gone."

"That doesn't exactly sound like breaking up," Claire pointed out.

"I wanted to let her down easy."

Then Claire slapped something down on the desk and asked, "So do you recognize this?" When she lifted her hand away, the military medal became visible, the side with the words Afghanistan Campaign and a map of Afghanistan on it.

Andrew stared at it. "Looks like a medal."

"Is it yours?"

He stood up and looked down at it. "Hard to say. Everyone who was in Afghanistan for longer than three months got one of those."

"Do you still have yours?"

"No." He shook his head. "I gave it to Tammy Lee."

"Why and when?"

"I sent it to her. I thought she would like it. It was before we broke up. Nothing special. But she liked to have things."

"Well, it appears she had it with her when she was burned. I found it in the ashes right where her body had been."

"Oh, geez. I had no idea she still had it." He sat down and put his head in his hands.

"I'd say she was carrying a torch for you," Amy remarked.

"Well, that's not what I wanted."

A knock came at the door and Amy opened it.

Mrs. Johansen stood there, looking in. She was wearing a denim jacket and jeans, and her blond hair was sticking up all over her head. "You found the ring?"

"We might have," Claire said.

Andrew stood up and offered his chair to the woman. She sat down without looking at him. Claire wondered if she had recognized him.

"I'm glad you could come down, Mrs. Johansen. I know this is hard. We found this ring and wondered if it might have been Tammy Lee's." She held out the bag for the woman to take.

She held the bag up close to her face and stared at it as if it would tell her something. "It looks like her ring. Small size and only a half-carat diamond. I can't be absolutely sure, but I bet the jeweler where they got it could tell. But I'm pretty sure that it is hers." She looked up. "Where did you find it?"

Without meaning to, Claire's eyes went to Andrew, who was standing behind Mrs. Johansen.

Mrs. Johansen turned and looked at him. "Andrew?" she said.

"Yes, ma'am," he said. "The ring was in my car."

Her voice shaking, Mrs. Johansen asked, "What did you do to my little girl?"

CHAPTER 16

Claire had both Andrew's car and Terry Whitman's vehicle brought in and called the crime lab to come and go over them for fingerprints and blood splatters. Also, she'd ask them to check out the Burning Boat crime scene more thoroughly.

After much thought, she decided she had to put Andrew on a leave of absence until the case was resolved. He hadn't lied to her about seeing Tammy Lee. He had told her that the first time they talked about her. The ring could have fallen off, or for that matter, Tammy Lee could have slipped it off and dropped it in his car on purpose—a good reason to see him again. And Claire didn't feel she had anything in the way of evidence or motive that told her Andrew might have killed Tammy Lee.

However, for the family and for the department, she felt like she needed to ask him to step down for a while.

She caught him as he was leaving work. They were standing in the hallway. When she told him that he would have to be on leave indefinitely, she thought for a moment that he was going to cry.

"You understand I have to do this, don't you?" she asked.

"Sure. I'd can me if I were in your place." He talked down to the floor, not looking up.

"You're not canned. Won't go on your record. View it as a break. But you might want to get some help."

"What do you mean?" Now he looked at her.

"I can put you in touch with a counselor."

"What for? I didn't do anything. I had nothing to do with Tammy Lee."

"You scrapped with Terry Whitman, which tells me you might have some anger issues. After all, you were in the war. You seem on edge to me, and I think it might do you good to talk to someone about this. No matter what your feelings were for Tammy Lee, her death has got to be hard on you, too."

He looked down again and nodded. "It is. I'm surprised, but I've been remembering the good times. She just liked life so much."

Claire felt the urge to reach out and pat his shoulder, but didn't think it was what a sheriff should do. Maybe if she had been just another deputy, his equal. But right now she wasn't.

"You want the name of that counselor?" she asked.

"Let me think about it. I just need to clear my head." He shifted his weight.

Claire stood in front of him, even though she could tell he wanted to go. Finally she said, "You know, I saw a therapist for a while. This job is hard on a person. We all can use some help."

"Yeah, I hear ya."

She stepped out of his way and then turned to watch him leave. Yes, she saw some hidden rage in him, but more than anything she saw a well of sadness.

❧

Amy drove out with the crime lab technicians to pick up Terry's car. His parents had said he was working for the next day or so and she could come any time to get it, although they didn't sound eager.

Once the car was loaded up on the transport, she drove a few blocks to talk to the Whitmans. They lived in a small apartment above a closed store downtown. The Chippewa River was just a block away. She parked on the street and pushed at the street door. There were buzzers, but the door was open. There was a very small entryway with six mailboxes, and then a steep flight of stairs.

She walked up the stairs and turned left to go down an uncarpeted hallway to the far end. Number Six: The Whitmans was hand-printed on a card stuck to the door. A Halloween sticker of a witch was stuck to the door above it. Amy wondered how many years it had been there.

Her knock was answered immediately by a woman that couldn't be fifty years old. She had dark red hair, a color that usually came from a bottle, and deep set blue eyes that looked worried. Small and stocky, she seemed soft. When the woman saw her uniform, she gave a quiet yelp—"Oh!"—and backed up into the apartment. Amy followed her in. "Mrs. Whitman?" she asked.

"Yes, I guess. But I've been divorced now for ten years. Just never bothered to change my name back. You can call me Betty."

The front windows looked out over main street and gave them a view of the river flowing by. It was one of the few nice things about the apartment. The couch looked more like a bed, piled with pillows and blankets and newspapers. A cat strolled through the room, but from the smell of the place, Amy guessed there were more.

"Betty, we took the car and we'll return it very soon."

"Terry will need it when he gets home."

"Just tell him to call us."

"Why are you doing this?" Betty asked. "Isn't it bad enough his fiancée dies, but then to blame him? I just don't get it. He's the last person who'd want to kill Tammy Lee. Why, he was crazy about her."

"How long had they been going out?"

"Long time now. I kept waiting for the wedding, but they wanted to save up. I can't help them much, you know."

"Was Terry jealous of her ever?"

Betty looked out the window. "He could be, you know. She was a little flirt sometimes, but nothing serious. They maybe had a tiff, but then the next day they were all lovey-dovey again. It's natural, that sort of thing."

Amy knew Claire wanted her to get some sense of Terry's history, if he had been in trouble as a boy. "How did Terry take your divorce?"

Betty looked startled. "Well, he was just a kid. His dad could be awful hard on him. Terry didn't say much, but I think he was glad his dad was gone. Still, they made him go see his dad every other week. He didn't complain, but I don't think he liked it much."

"Was he a good kid?"

"Oh, yeah. Terry was fine. Didn't do that well in school, but could always fix things. He just didn't like to sit still, was his problem. He wanted to be on the go. That's why working for the railroad is perfect for him."

"He ever get in trouble when he was a teenager?"

"Oh, you know, the way kids do. He got caught shoplifting some candy bars one time, I remember. Boy, I laid into him about that. Then he'd stay out all night as he got older. I did worry about him. But he turned out fine. I just don't know how he's going to get over Tammy Lee's death."

Another cat came out from under the couch and rubbed against Amy's legs. "Nice cats."

"Oh, they're my loves. I have six of them. But can't let the landlord know. He said two's the limit. They tend to hide when anyone comes over—which is good. They must like you. Terry doesn't care for them much. He'll take a swat at them if they come too close."

"Did they have a date set for the wedding?"

"I thought they did. They kept saying it was going to be the first week in the new year, but then Terry said something about Tammy Lee changing her mind again. That girl, not very steady. I was ready, though. I picked out a dress and everything. I guess I'll never wear it now."

She picked up a cat and put her face in its fur, tears filling her eyes. "I was so looking forward to that wedding. It would have been a happy time."

−

Grandma was sleeping in the La-Z-Boy recliner. She slept in that chair a lot these days. Doug wasn't even sure she used her bed anymore. She didn't move around much, and when she did it looked like every step hurt her.

Not like before, when he was a kid and she was a bundle of energy, cooking for everyone, doing laundry, taking care of the farm, the chickens, gardening.

Doug looked around and saw that the farm was just about done for, and she could hardly manage the house anymore. The floors were dirty, the counters stacked with papers and dishes. He took out the garbage and couldn't even fit it in the garbage can. She must be forgetting to bring the can out to the road for pickup.

His time here was almost done. He had slept some and eaten some good meals. He felt ready for his last step. But he worried about Grandma, with no one to care for her or even worry about her. She had always been so good to him.

When he got back in the house, he went right to the phone. He dialed a number he had memorized. It was late enough that Andrew should be home from work. If one of his parents answered, he'd just hang up.

"Sticklers," Andrew answered.

"Hey, Stick-man. How's it blowing?"

"Doug, I've been trying to reach you. Where are you?"

"I told you I'd come for you. I told you I'd check in when I was feeling better. So here I am."

"Are you feeling better?"

Doug looked at his grandma sleeping in the recliner, then he glanced over at the gun leaning in the corner of the kitchen. "Yeah, I'm stoked."

"What for?"

"You know, our little get-together."

"You want me to come to where you are?"

"No need, my man. I've got it all mapped out. You know I'm good at that. Mapping the territory. I've reconnaissanced. I know where you live. I know where you work. I even know where your little friend is."

Silence, then Andrew asked, "What little friend?"

"That one you talked about—Tammy. Showed me her picture when we first met. Cute as they come. And I bet she comes pretty often, hey, Stick-man."

"What do you know about her?"

"Just what you told me. But when can we get together?"

"The sooner the better. I've got some days off work."

"Okay, I'll call you when I get closer to your place. Hasta la vista, Stick-man." He hung up the phone even though he could hear Andrew was still talking. Let him talk. Let him try to persuade him to not do what he planned on doing. But a vow is a vow, and he knew he had to carry it out.

CHAPTER 17

"You have to remember, this took place in a far-off land with mountains taller than the clouds and ravines deeper than the sea." Andrew watched Meg's face in the shadowy light of the campfire. He felt like he was telling her a fairy story, and to her it might be, but to him it was more real than where he was sitting right now, and would always and ever be a nightmare.

"The people who live there," he continued, "it's hard to describe them—how much they are like us—and how different. We were there to fight for them and they hated our guts.

"Most of the time we stay huddled in the outpost, cleaning our guns, smoking, trying not to think. You make friends, good friends, with guys you would never even talk to normally, never even know. That's how Doug and I and this other guy named Brian came together. We just hooked up. We palled around. We almost always went out on forays together. We were tight, very tight."

Meg nodded. "Good buddies."

"But it's more than just that. It's like we counted on each other to stay alive. More like brothers, maybe even more than that. And we watched out for each other, always. And everything was a clue as to what would happen next. If the moon was full, if the wind was from the south, if it rained, which it hardly ever did—everything was a clue to be read as to what our fate might be. If we would make it."

"But you did." Meg leaned into him.

"Yes, I did. But Doug's in pretty rough shape. Or at least, he was last I saw him. He went off the deep end. Couldn't sleep, wouldn't eat, carried his gun everywhere he went, slept with it. Finally the higher ups noticed and he got pulled. Sent to Germany. Haven't seen him since."

"And Brian?" Meg asked.

"Yeah." Andrew knew to keep it short. "He's dead. Died out there in the mountains. Fell off a cliff and got shot on the way down. He died and he died."

"I'm so sorry," Meg said, touching his face.

Why was he telling her this? He didn't want to break down in front of her. Instead he pulled her to him and rolled back onto the sleeping bag. The wind swept through the trees above them, the moon was edging over the tops of the branches, all the signs were in his favor. He needed to feel something other than the pain and guilt he had been living with since he got home.

He needed Meg to help him.

He kissed her, not gentle, with all the hunger he had ever felt. "Please," he asked. "Please let me."

Her mouth opened and he drank her. Then he pulled at her clothes, needing to feel her skin. She kept opening and he kept moving deeper into her. She was Meg, and then she was more. She was the earth, a warm place to be safe, he wanted to be in her.

He heard her cry out as he entered her, but he couldn't stop. What he was after was the explosion that covered everything for a while, that took over the world for moments and made him forget. It came so fast he wasn't ready for it: the wind, the leaves, the stars, all swept through him and then he collapsed on top of her.

Quietness descended. He wouldn't have known she was crying if he hadn't felt her tears wet his hand.

"Hey," he whispered to her. "Are you okay?"

"Yeah," she said, but her voice quivered.

He wrapped his arms around her. "Wasn't it good for you?"

"I just wasn't quite ready for it."

"I'm sorry."

"No, don't be. I wanted it, too. I did. It's just that I, well, I hadn't done it before."

Andrew sat up and looked down at her. The glimpses of her white body shone in the firelight in the mess of her clothes. He reached out and touched her belly. "Your first time? Oh, baby, I would have been more careful if I'd known. I'm so sorry."

"No, it was fine."

But he could hear in her voice it wasn't, and he felt like he had failed again. He had taken her with no thought, no contraception, no carefulness. What was the matter with him? It was like he wasn't human anymore, just an animal surviving. He turned away from her and looked at the fire.

To be burnt to nothing in a fire, that wouldn't be a bad way to go.

∾

When Fred from the crime lab called, Claire was on her way home. It had been a very long day, and now that she was acting sheriff she could never turn her phone off. Not that she often did as a deputy, either.

"What have you got?" she asked, no wasting time on pleasantries.

"There's certainly evidence of Ms. Johansen in Whitman's car. But we knew that going in to the search. Long blond hair is in both the front and back seat. Don't know it's hers, but we're guessing. Fingerprints galore, those we matched." Fred paused and then said, "The weird thing is there is a long blond hair in the trunk too. No blood or anything—we used the luminal spray, didn't see a thing. But there is this one long hair in a rather odd place."

"She wasn't necessarily bleeding when she was killed. And she could have put something in the trunk and left a hair behind."

"Yes, but we found it toward the back of the trunk, not near the front where it would be likely to be if she were just getting something in or out of it. And it was caught on a piece of metal that holds the back seats in place. Looking at where it is, I'm guessing the person would have had to have climbed in the trunk."

"Okay, I'll follow up on this. Thanks."

"Good luck. I'll send you all the fingerprint info and the hair samples tomorrow."

When Claire hung up, she sat and thought about Terry. Amy had been watching his movements, and he had just left on the train for an overnight run to Chicago. He'd be back tomorrow. The hair was inconclusive, but definitely meant he should be looked at more carefully. Plus, if what Andrew said was true and Tammy Lee was thinking of dumping Terry, that would certainly give him motive.

She walked over to Amy's desk and gave her the news.

Amy shook her head. "I'm not getting a good feeling from this guy. No one I have talked to has had much good to say about him."

"Still not enough reason to arrest him." Claire said. "But why don't you do a little more sniffing, go to that bar he frequents, see what you can learn, and then when he gets back tomorrow, let's bring him in for a little talk. I think it's time he sees the inside of this place and we have a little face time with him."

❧

They sat down to dinner together across from each other at the kitchen table. Doug remembered they almost always ate in the kitchen, even though there was a dining room with a big table and six chairs. Only on holidays did they eat in the dining room. Just more cozy in the kitchen, Grandma would say.

She had made scrambled eggs and boiled some potatoes. It wasn't much of a meal, and still she hardly ate any of it.

"Grandma, don't you have any meat in the house?"

"Oh, Dougie, it's so dear. I only have some social security to live on, and that's gotta last me the whole month. Barely pays the bills. It's hard getting old and sick. No fun."

It was not like his grandmother to complain. But when he looked over at her, he wondered if she was really the same woman anymore. Like him. You go through something and it changes you so much, you're never the same. You can't go back to what you once were.

He remembered how easily he had moved through life in high school. He had been a star football player, all the girls wanted to go out with him. Now he was damaged inside and out, and no woman wanted anything to do with him. It was like they smelled the dead on him, the dying he was doing inside.

Seemed the same with Grandma. She was just shuffling through life, moving from the toilet to the recliner to the kitchen and back again. Not really living. Just waiting to die.

"I'm sorry, Grandma. Wish I could stay and take care of you."

She patted his hand. "Don't be sorry for me. I've had a good life, most of it. Just wish it were over, that's all. I'm no good for anyone now, and can't even pay my doctor bills. I'm afraid they're going to take the house."

Doug looked around the old place. He could tell that nothing had been done on the upkeep for years. Windows were cracked, paint peeling off the clapboard, gutters hanging loose from the roof. But she had lived in it most of her life.

"Do you want to move?" he asked.

"No, I want to die right here. Is that too much to ask?" She got up and started to clear the table.

"You go lie down, Grandma. I'll take care of this." Doug ran a sink full of hot water and used the last few drops in the bottle of dishwashing soap. He washed all the dishes and the pots and pans that had accumulated on the stove. He wiped down the stove and the refrigerator and the table. He thought of washing the floor, but then thought, what's the use? At least the kitchen was clean. People wouldn't think she had neglected her duties.

When he peeked into the living room, she was sleeping in her recliner. Her face had smoothed out and her hands were folded in her lap. He had always loved her and this was one last thing he could do for her.

He walked up the stairs to his room to get the gun.

CHAPTER 18

Andrew hated not working. He'd lie in bed as long as he could stand it, then get up and go downstairs and drink coffee with his mom. She would make him some eggs without even asking what he wanted. The radio would be on, giving the weather report, so important in farming. After that, classical music would fill the room and she would clean up the kitchen, humming softly to herself, not usually matching the music but playing off of it.

His mom never asked what he was going to do—either with his day or with his life. It was one of the many things he liked about her. She knew how to let a man be alone. Sometimes he'd wander out and try to help his dad, but there wasn't that much to do. Harvest was over and his dad was usually tinkering away on the old tractor or some other piece of machinery, just to pass the time. He didn't really want any help, and Andrew wasn't that good at it.

After breakfast Andrew pulled on a jacket and went outside, but rather than try to find his dad he decided to walk the fields, see if he could scare up some pheasants just to see them fly their bullet-flight low over the broken cornstalks.

He still felt horrible about last night with Meg. She had assured him that he had done nothing wrong, that she had wanted it too, but had just been taken by surprise. Yeah, I guess, your first time and the dink of a guy doesn't even know enough to take it slow. Next time he would do it right. If there was a next time.

She had kissed him as sweetly as ever when he dropped her off a few blocks from her house, but he wondered. She was so young. She knew so little of what life could be like. Her mother was only trying to protect her from men like him. Maybe Meg wouldn't want to see him again.

Maybe he should leave her alone. It would be better for her. He had little to offer anyone right now.

He walked to the edge of the field, a place where he knew he could get pretty good cell phone reception. He needed to talk to Doug, find out what he was doing. Maybe they should meet and talk things over. He owed at least that to Doug. After all, more than just Brian had died that day on the ridge.

Andrew dialed Doug's cell phone number, which he knew by heart. He didn't expect to get through.

The phone rang and rang. Andrew counted up to ten and then disconnected. No voice mail, nothing. He'd expected this result, but he had hoped, since Doug had called him yesterday, that he might have left the phone on and maybe even would answer it.

Then Andrew remembered that the number Doug had called from yesterday had not been the cell phone number. He looked it up and hit dial. The phone rang three times, then someone answered with a very tentative, "Hello."

It wasn't Doug, but it was a man.

"Yes, is Doug there?"

"Doug who?" the man asked.

"Doug Nelson."

The man cleared his voice. "This is the Nelson residence, but I don't think Doug is here. It's his grandmother's house. She's been killed. I need to call the police. Just came over to drop off some eggs for her. Was Doug here?"

"I think so. He called me from there."

"Well, I'm sorry to be the bearer of such sad tidings, but it looks like someone came in the house and shot his grandma. She always left the door unlocked. We all do. That way I can check on her. Who are you?"

"I'm—" Andrew wasn't sure what to say. "I guess I'm a friend of Doug's."

"Well, let him know if you talk to him. She hasn't been that close to her family in a long time."

"I'm sorry."

"Yeah, she was doing poorly, but she didn't deserve this. She had nothing worth stealing, that's for sure."

Andrew hung up the phone. Now his number would be recorded as having called her. And he knew that Doug had been there the night before. What the hell was going on with Doug? Would he have killed his grandmother?

Doug had always wanted control in a world that had gone crazy. He was the one who was always planning what the three of them would do after their tour of duty.

Doug was the one who had persuaded them to take the vow.

Andrew knew he had to get in touch with him before anything else happened.

In a way, he was responsible for it all.

എ

"There he is," Amy said, pointing out to Claire the young man dressed in a jean jacket with a skull cap pulled down right over his forehead. Terry Whitman didn't strike her as an aggressive man, but that was to be seen.

They had been sitting in a squad car at the train station, waiting for the train from Chicago to pull in. The train was almost an hour late. Claire was well aware of this, because she had already called Rich once to tell him to hold dinner. Depending on how their conversation went with Terry Whitman, she warned him that she might not even get home before midnight.

Claire and Amy stepped out of the car and approached Terry Whitman from both sides.

"Hey, Terry, Deputy Amy Shroeder. We need to talk to you about some new evidence we've found about Tammy Lee."

He stopped and looked at her. "You got some info on Tammy Lee? Well, it's about time. I talked to her folks last night and they're torn up about this."

"Yes, I can imagine." Claire took his arm to steer him toward the squad car.

He shook her off. "I can talk, but not now, man. I just got off my shift. I'm beat. I need some sleep."

"So you don't want to hear about Tammy Lee." Claire stepped closer to him. He wasn't much bigger than she was.

"Yeah, sure I do. But I need some shut-eye. Can't I call you later?"

"Terry, we went through your car."

He bent his head slightly, then came up for air. "So?"

"So we found something." Claire thought she'd let him dangle a bit. See what he did with this information.

"Like I said, Tammy Lee was in my car all the time. So what if you found her fingerprints or whatever." He tried to walk away from them.

"We need to talk now." Claire grabbed his arm, and this time wasn't so gentle about it. She wheeled him toward the squad car. Amy already had the back door open. He ducked his head and sank into the back, looking like he was both resigned and exhausted.

"What did you find?" he asked when she started driving.

"We'll talk at the station," Claire told him.

"I already talked to her." He pointed at Amy. "She knows what happened. What about Andrew Stickler? He's the guy. He wanted her back, but she was having none of it. She told me so herself."

"Do you know what happened to her ring?" Claire asked, curious what he would say.

He sunk further down in the seat and stared out the window. "She said she lost it. She said it slipped off her finger. I couldn't believe it. How can you lose a real diamond engagement ring? That was like a month's salary for me."

Claire didn't say anything more. She drove back up to Durand, Amy sitting quietly next to her, Terry dozing in the back seat.

She turned to Amy. "I want you to go to the bar where Terry was the other night when he got home. Ask around. See what kind of mood he was in, find out if he talked to anyone about Tammy Lee."

Amy nodded.

Claire didn't like the guy. She knew that shouldn't matter in how she went at the case, but she couldn't help not liking him. He was arrogant and cocky, and under it all, she was sure, very insecure. A bad combination. Even his reaction to the lost ring showed his anger. She just hoped Tammy Lee hadn't been the victim of an eruption that could have resulted.

❧

Meg grabbed the keys of the pickup. She didn't care what her mom wanted her to do, she was going to see Andrew. He had called and hadn't sounded very good. He was stuck at his parents' house. He had tried to tell her something about a friend's grandma dying, then something about a vow, but then it sounded like he had started crying. That had scared her. Why was he crying about someone else's relative?

He had tried to explain. She told him she would be right over.

It didn't matter that a storm was moving across Lake Pepin, a roiling, seething monster of a storm that was already shooting off spears of tearing light that shattered the sky. This conversation could not happen over the phone. She needed to be there with him.

In normal weather, it would take her twenty minutes to get to his house. Tonight, if the rain let loose, it was hard to tell—maybe she would race the storm across the land and beat it. She set off in the pickup, keeping an eye on the weather to the west.

Within minutes, the wind caught up with her. She could feel herself wrestling with the steering wheel. The rain came down so hard she could only see the road for a moment after the wipers cleared the glass. She watched for the yellow line, drove slow but steady.

Then ahead of her something cracked, and a tree came lashing down only yards in the front of the truck. She stepped on the brakes and the truck came to a rest, held in the tree branches, but unhurt.

What was she doing? How important was Andrew to her? What was she risking by seeing him again?

Meg climbed out of the car, went around to the other side of the tree, and started to pull at the tree's branches. The tree wasn't that big, but it was heavy. She was barely able to move it a few feet, but it was enough so that the truck was no longer tangled with tree limbs.

Soaked to the skin, she climbed into the truck, backed up and skirted around the tree. She turned down a road leading away from the lake and the storm abated, sheltered in the bluffs. When her teeth started chattering, she thought to turn on the heat, blower on high.

By the time she got to the Stickler farmhouse, she had dried off a bit, but her clothes were still damp and her hair was hanging in strands down her neck. The rain had eased up but she knew she would get wet again, running to the back door of the house. As she jumped out of the truck and slammed the door, she saw Andrew walking across the yard with an umbrella in his hand, held up high. She ran to him and he grabbed her tight with his free hand. They kissed, a wet kiss mixed with rain.

"Thanks for coming," he said.

"No prob."

"I've got two beers waiting for us in the barn. It will be a little more private there." Still holding her around the waist, he walked her to the open barn door. A few feet in, a table was set up with two bales of hay pushed close for chairs. Two bottles of Leinenkugel beer were already open.

"So fancy," she said.

"Nothing but the best. Plus, this way we can watch the storm."

They sat down close to each other on one bale and tipped their beer bottles together. After they drank, Meg wiped his hair back from his face and asked, "So tell me what is going on?"

Andrew picked at the label of his beer bottle and said, "I don't know where to start. It's just so hard to explain what happened over there."

Meg guessed he meant Afghanistan. She stayed quiet.

"Life was this weird combination of really boring and bone-sizzling scary. We spent most of our time waiting for something to happen and then when it did we just hoped we'd come through it alive. I got to be pretty good friends with these two guys—I told you about them—Doug and Brian. One night we were goofing around and Doug said, let's take a vow. We were drinking and knew something was up. It had grown kinda quiet around us and that meant some action would happen in the next day or two. So he says, yeah, let's vow that we all three make it out of this, or none of us do. That we go down together or we leave together. I can't explain why, but it seemed like a good idea at the time. Like we were linked, and that way we'd be stronger. So we vowed we'd be in it together, praying we'd all come out alive."

Meg took a swig of her beer and nodded. "A vow."

"We swore it on our hearts. I know it sounds weird, but it seemed like the thing to do. The next day the three of us, along with some other guys, are sent off into the hills to find a hidden treasure—they claim they've got the mother of all ammos tucked away in a cave.

"We're the scouts. We're not supposed to engage. Just try to light the way for the other guys. We walk for what seems like hours, carefully checking all around us as we go. We almost get to the cave when I hear something. It's like a chatter, like an animal that's mad, we're in its territory. I think it's nothing, but Doug blows. He shoots at it—whatever it is—like he can't help it.

"Now we're in trouble. If anyone is out there, they know where we are. The other guys behind us drop back. We're stranded close to the cave. Before I hear them, before I see them, I feel them. They're surrounding us. We're up on a high ridge, one side a sheer drop-off and the other side dense brush."

He stopped, and his hand covered his eyes for a moment.

"Are you sure you want to tell me this?" Meg asked.

"Please," he said, and then continued, "I need to explain what happened to someone. It's hard to capture how bad it was. Then it happened. Like at some secret signal, the world exploded. I was hugging the earth. Doug was firing back, like a crazy man, he was standing and shooting as if they couldn't see him, like he was invisible.

"Then it got worse. Doug got hit. I saw him go down. I was crawling over to where he was when I saw Brian start to go over the cliff. I grabbed his hand and he pulled me to the edge. He was dangling and I was holding on. They were shooting at us. Then he fell, and his body got ripped up by shots on the way down. He bounced on the rocks like a rag doll."

Andrew was shaking. Meg stood above him and wrapped her arms around his neck, pulling him into her. She wanted to know how he had made it. She wanted to know what this had to do with the grandmother. But she just held him until he calmed. He took one of her hands and turned it over and kissed the palm.

"Thanks," he said.

"I'm sorry," she said.

"What for?"

"That you had to go through that."

"Well, I made it. Somehow I made it through. I dug into a bush, dragged Doug in with me, and the other men came pouring in and took over. I didn't come out. I stayed in there, hidden, until all the shooting was over. Doug was bad. A bullet had clipped his head. He was bleeding like a stuck pig. We got him out of there, and they choppered him out that night. I was sent home two weeks later. My last tour of duty was over. I don't know if I could have gone back."

"What about Doug?"

"I haven't seen him since. He's called me a few times, but he sounds pretty strange. Talks about the vow. How we left Brian behind. He wants to see me. Called last night. When I tried to get back to him this morning, I figured out he was calling from his grandma's. She doesn't live too far from here, down Fountain City way. I called there and some neighbor answered and said Doug was gone."

"Oh," Meg said, knowing there was more.

"And that his grandmother was dead. Someone shot her."

CHAPTER 19

When Terry took his cap off, Claire could see that he was a little older than she had thought. His hair was starting to thin at the front of his head. He rubbed at his eyes and then stared around the room. "Nice office," he said.

"It's just temporary."

"So you're not really the sheriff?"

"For now," Claire said, then wondered why she did that. He didn't need to know this information, and she was the one that should be asking the questions. "Let me just get this time frame straight. When was the last time you saw Tammy Lee?"

"Thursday night, like I already told that other woman deputy. I got off work, had a drink at the bar, then we hung out for a while."

"Anything happen?"

"Not really. I'm not much good after a shift. Tammy Lee wanted to party, but I wasn't up for it."

"Is this when she told you about the ring?"

"Naw, she told me that while I was working. Wish she would have waited. Got me all riled up. Maybe it's stupid, but it just don't seem right that she would lose the ring before we even got married. Like it's a bad omen." He stopped talking, his eyes dropping down to the hat in his hands. "I guess maybe it was."

"Were you mad at her?"

"Sure, I was mad. Who wouldn't be."

"You ever get violent with her."

"Not much. Maybe once, I punched her. But when she'd have too much to drink she could get nasty. She'd slap me and call me names. But usually she wasn't like that." He leaned down and his voice was muffled. "I still can't believe she's gone."

"Did you think she really lost the ring?"

He looked up. "What do you mean?"

"Did it ever occur to you that she might have taken it off on purpose, maybe she didn't want to wear it anymore?"

"Sometimes she would tease me, say it was over, but the next day everything would be all right again. Until that Andrew came back. He's the one you should be talking to, not me. She said he wanted her back. Thinks he's so big just cause he went over and fought in the war. And he has a temper. You know he slugged me out in the parking lot."

"Yes, I know that. I also know that you hit him, too."

"A guy's got to defend himself."

Claire reached into the drawer of the desk and pulled out a plastic bag. She handed it over to Terry. "Is this the ring?"

"Hard to see through this plastic," he complained.

Claire reached into her pocket and handed him a pair of plastic gloves. "Put these on and you can take it out."

Reluctantly, he snapped the gloves on and then opened the bag. Holding the ring in his hands, he said, "I'm pretty sure it is. Where did you find it?"

His question stopped Claire. Usually she had a questioning all thought out, but this was rather informal. They weren't charging him with anything, yet. "She dropped it in a friend's car."

"Whose?" Terry asked, dropping the ring back in the bag.

"What would you have done if Tammy Lee had left you for Andrew?"

"I'd have killed them both."

෬

Andrew roused slowly as he heard some music coming from next to the bed. At first he thought it was the clock radio alarm waking him for work, but then he remembered he was on leave. He realized it was his phone in time to grab it and mumble, "Hello," before it went to voice mail.

"Stick-man, Dougie here."

"Doug, wha' time is it?"

"I dunno. Late, or early."

"What's up? You coming my way?"

"Yeah, just wondering if we could hook up tomorrow."

"Yeah, that'd be perfect." Andrew thought quickly. He didn't want Doug to come to his parents' house, not until he was sure that he wasn't going to be too crazy. "You know where Fort St. Antoine is?"

"I already told you I've been doing my recon. Saw that sweetheart of yours."

"What're you talking about?" Andrew thought of Meg.

"That Tammy Lee. She is one stacked woman. Feisty, too."

"When did you see her?"

"I don't remember exactly. Sometime last week. Before I came to my grandma's. I was getting pretty tired. Things kinda all mix together in my mind."

Andrew didn't want to scare him off, so he decided not to ask him anything more about Tammy Lee. He needed to get Doug, to meet him. That was what was important now. When he was face to face with him, he could ask him if anything happened to Tammy Lee or his grandmother.

"Sure. Well, there's a bar, the Fort, right on the corner of Highway 35 and Main Street. I'll meet you there. What time can you be there?"

"I'm probably going to sleep in, and I'm still a ways away. Haven't been sleeping that good. Let's say around eight tomorrow night."

"Where've you been?"

"Around."

Andrew thought about all Doug wasn't saying. "Any place in particular?"

"I stopped off to visit my grandma."

"Oh, yeah. How's she doing?"

"Not so good. She's got that cancer pretty bad. But I think she was happy to see me."

Andrew just couldn't bring himself to give Doug the news of his grandmother's death over the phone. He knew Doug had been close to her. Plus, he wanted to see his face when he told him. He needed to know if Doug already knew about the death. "That's good. See you at eight."

&

When Amy walked into the bar, she realized she hadn't been there in quite a while. She guessed that's what happened when you settled down and didn't need to go trolling the local haunts to find some guy. Looking around at the blue air, the rumpled hair, the hunting jackets and baseball caps, the sagging shoulders of the men lined up at the bar, she was so happy she didn't need to visit very often.

She was still in her uniform, so she got the stares and then the quick looks away. All of the men probably had something in their past they weren't proud of, some bill they hadn't paid, some driving violation they hoped no one had seen.

There was a stool open in the middle of the pack and she walked over, sat down and ordered a Leinie on tap. "I'm off duty," she explained to the bartender.

"It's okay with me," he said. "On the house." He set it down in front of her.

She slid a couple bucks across the bar—he could use them to pay for the beer or as a tip, didn't matter to her. "You know Terry Whitman?"

Bartender scratched his head. "Terry? Short guy? Works for the railroad?"

"That's the one."

"I've served him. Not much of a talker. Comes in, has a few brewskis after work, then he leaves."

"Anyone here a friend of his?"

Bartender looked up and down the bar, shaking his head, then he looked back to a booth and then pointed. "That guy knows him. I think they work together."

Amy walked over to the booth. A man with steel-gray hair cut short and a weathered face looked up at her without turning his head. He had both hands around his beer glass. "You looking for me?" he asked.

"Not really," she said to reassure him. Then, without waiting to be asked, she sat down across from him. "Not you. I'm wondering what you can tell me about Terry Whitman."

"Not much. Cocky guy. Does his job. Don't know him that well." He lowered his head to take a sip of beer, barely lifting the glass up. He seemed dog tired.

"You just get off a shift?" she asked.

"Yeah."

"You seem exhausted."

"Yeah, the shifts aren't getting any easier." He kept his gaze lowered at the table as if he didn't want her to be there.

"I know what you mean," Amy said, pointing at her uniform even though he wasn't looking at her. "I just got off too."

"So this isn't official?"

She ignored that question. "You heard that Terry's fiancée died?"

"Something like that."

"You ever meet Tammy Lee?"

"Sort of. She'd be waiting for him here in the bar most nights he got off. They'd hang around for a while, you know. We didn't socialize or anything, but I'd see them together."

"Was she here last Thursday night?"

"Yeah, I'm pretty sure she was."

"What state was she in?"

"Kind of happy. She was tying one on, if you ask me."

"Was that usual?"

"Not unusual."

Amy now really understood the phrase 'it was like pulling teeth.' This guy had a clenched jaw; hard to get anything out of him. "Did you notice anything going on between the two of them?"

"Well, they didn't leave together."

"Oh?"

"Yeah, she left first. Then Terry finished his drink, hung out maybe another fifteen minutes or so and left."

"How did he seem?"

"Like usual. Tired, a little pissed off. But that was Terry."

"Do you think Terry could have killed her?"

He took another slurp of his beer, then looked up at her for the second time. "Don't know, but wouldn't surprise me."

CHAPTER 20

Rich wasn't sure when Claire was coming home, and for once he didn't feel like waiting for her to call to find out. Since she had taken over as sheriff, her schedule was more packed and erratic than ever. Often she would come home an hour or two after he and Meg had eaten and stand by the refrigerator, eating leftovers, not even bothering to sit down.

He felt like having someone else cook for him, and he felt like eating a hamburger. Meg had told him she was going out to eat and then ran upstairs to get ready, so he didn't have to worry about her. He had a feeling she was going to meet Andrew, but he didn't ask and she didn't say.

He decided to walk down to the Fort, a small café bar right in downtown Fort St. Antoine. It wasn't even a mile away. Not that he needed the exercise—pheasant season was going strong and he was exhausted every day from the work—but it was a nice night, and in October you didn't know how many of those you'd have left. Winter could come along any time. No one in his generation would ever get over the Halloween snowstorm in 1992 that dropped over two feet of snow in a day and half, most of which never melted all winter long. Just more snow piled on top of it.

But tonight, the air was crisp and snappy, like biting into an apple. The sun was leaving the sky a bit sooner every night and he hated to see it go, but there was still a bit of dusk left in the west, over the lake. Not much traffic along Highway 35. The leafers didn't usually come out mid-week, and the colors hadn't been that good this year.

He could see the Fort ahead of him, the big red Texaco star all lit up from when it had also been a gas station. No one but a fool would ever take that sign away. It was a classic, and right in keeping with this old rivertown.

When he walked in the Fort, he saw the place was nearly empty. Two kids were playing pool while their parents had a beer. A lone man ordered something at the far end of the bar.

The man turned when Rich came up to the bar, and Rich saw who it was.

"Andrew, how's it going?"

"Hey, Rich. Not as good as it could be."

"Sorry to hear that."

"No one's fault but my own."

"Sometimes it's just like that."

"Want to grab a booth?" Rich asked.

"No." Andrew lowered his head, then shook it. "I'm meeting somebody here in a bit. But thanks."

Rich ordered a burger and wondered who Andrew might be meeting, and if he would feel compelled to tell Claire about this rendezvous. He hoped not.

❧

Andrew had made a hard decision. He had to tell Meg they needed to quit seeing each other, at least until this investigation was over. And preferably until he got his feet back on the ground emotionally. He was still upset about the way he had pushed her into having sex with him, assuming she wanted it when he did. If he had even taken the time to think about what she wanted.

Maybe he did need to check into the VA and see a therapist again. He had hoped he could avoid that—certainly no badge of courage in the armed services, but he knew that PTSD was turning up in a third of returning vets. What made him think he would be so lucky as to avoid that curse completely?

When he looked around the bar, he saw Rich Haggard walk into the Fort. Rich was a good guy, but Andrew didn't know him very well and couldn't be sure he wouldn't let Claire know that Meg and he had been seen together.

He hoped Meg would get here before Doug. He wanted to get that talk with her out of the way before he tackled whatever Doug had going on in his crazy brain. One thing about Doug—at least the Doug he had known in Afghanistan—the guy couldn't lie to save his life. If he had done something to his grandmother, he would tell Andrew.

Andrew heard the door bang shut and turned to see Doug walk in. He looked rugged, like he had been out on duty for days and hadn't had time to shave or bath. He certainly didn't look like he was in the service anymore, as his hair was down to his shoulders.

Yet there seemed to be less of him.

Doug had been a pretty bulky guy in Afghanistan, working out on weights every day, eating more than his fair share of the awful grub. He had dwindled since he had come stateside.

Andrew raised his hand. "Doug, over here."

Doug nodded, then scanned the room before he walked across it. Still working the area. When he got closer, Andrew could see his eyes were bloodshot and wary, and the scar on the side of his head.

Andrew stood up from his stool and reached for Doug. Doug pulled back for a moment, then grabbed onto Andrew and squeezed him hard.

"Too long, buddy," Andrew said.

"Yeah, man. I didn't know if I'd ever see you again. After what happened over there."

Andrew wasn't ready to talk about what happened in Afghanistan. He wanted to get some food and drink into Doug before they got into it.

"How does a burger sound?"

"Yeah, I could go for that," Doug said, sliding onto a stool, but still checking the room.

Andrew ordered two burgers with fries. "You want a brew?"

"Sure, whatever they have."

When the two glasses of Leinenkugel's came, they tapped them together and Doug's eyes started to water. "Who'd a thunk we'd ever be here like this. Just normal guys drinking a beer."

"I knew we'd make it."

"Yeah, but Brian didn't."

Andrew didn't want to talk about Brian. Not yet. "What you been doing with yourself?"

Doug shook his head. "Not much. For a while they had me on so many meds I couldn't see straight. So I took myself off all that crap, which made me go berserk. Then my folks threw me out."

"Sorry to hear that."

"Yeah, they said I screamed too much at night and drank too much during the day. Probably right."

"So you were at your grandmother's?"

Doug jerked, then asked, "How'd you know that?"

"Caller ID."

"I just stopped by for a moment to say hi. Used her phone."

"How's she doing?"

"Not great. Going downhill. Wants to die."

Before Andrew could ask him anything more, the hamburgers came. He watched as Doug started to wolf his burger down. He ate like he hadn't eaten in a week and might never eat again.

☙

Meg wasn't sure where Rich had gone; probably feeding the few remaining pheasants. She grabbed a jean jacket and wrapped a blue scarf she had just finished knitting around her neck a few times. If Andrew liked it, maybe she'd give it to him. She was glad her mom wasn't home from work yet. Made it easier not to have to avoid or lie if they asked her where she was going. Who she would be with.

Andrew hadn't sounded that good on the phone. Kind of distant. But the more she knew of what he had gone through over in Afghanistan, the more she understood him. And the more she felt drawn to him, like she could do him some good, help him through this hard time.

As much as she didn't believe in the war he had fought, she respected him for doing what he saw was his duty. She didn't want to be one of those people who shunned a returning soldier.

She was running late so she climbed in the pickup to drive downtown, something she rarely did.

Before she backed out of the driveway, she glanced in the mirror and fluffed her hair. She imagined Andrew's hands in her curls. But tonight she wouldn't let things go that far—not that she regretted having sex with him. She just wanted to get to know him better and have it happen under better conditions, like in a real bed. Some place where she might enjoy it more.

Meg drove down Highway 35 and knew they were taking a risk by meeting at the Fort. If her mom found out about it, she was just going to say that they ran into each other. What could her mom do? Ground her? A couple more months and she'd be gone. As excited as she was about going to college, she wondered if she would keep seeing Andrew.

She saw Andrew's Jeep and was glad he was already there. Nice to have the guy be on time and waiting. Showed he was attentive.

When she pushed through the door, everyone in the place looked at her. She saw Andrew right away, up at the bar with another guy. Then she noticed Rich. He waved at her and turned back to his food. She'd talk to him later. See if she could persuade him to not tell her mom.

Andrew stood up and took her arm as she walked up. "Hey, Meg. You look great. I want you to meet a friend of mine." He gestured toward the scruffy young man next to him. Meg guessed he was about her age. "This is Doug. We were over in Afghanistan together."

"Doug," Meg said and held out her hand.

He shied away from her, but ducked his head in a kind of acknowledgement. "Hey, Meg."

She let her hand drop. "Nice to meet you."

"Doug's grandmother lives near here, so he called when he was visiting her. I told you about that. I asked him to join us. I hope that's okay."

"Sure. Where did your grandmother live?" Meg asked.

Doug's eyes dropped to the floor. "On the farm. Down near Fountain City. She was the only family I had left, just about."

Meg thought it was odd he didn't say anything about his grandmother's death.

"His grandmother hadn't been doing that well," Andrew explained.

"Oh, I'm sorry. I heard she died."

Doug lifted his head and his eyes were filled with tears. "She wanted to. She was just too tired to go on living. That's what she told me."

CHAPTER 21

Claire walked into an empty house. She could tell because there was no smell of food being cooked in the kitchen, the radio wasn't on, and Meg wasn't lounging on the couch, reading or watching TV. Odd to have the house be so quiet.

Claire let her coat fall off of her shoulders. She was almost too tired to hang it up. She wanted this investigation to be over, to get back to petty crimes like brawling drunks, and teenagers TPing houses. A robbery would even be nice. Something she could sink her teeth into, but where no one got hurt.

The bones of Tammy Lee Johansen haunted her. So little left of the young woman, just the ivory structure that had held up her body only days ago.

Claire sat down at the kitchen table and rubbed her face. She knew she had to eat. She looked around to see if Rich had left her a note, but there was nothing. Unusual. Maybe he was mad at her about something. She knew that he wasn't terrifically happy about her taking over as sheriff, even if it was temporary.

She had decided to hold Terry Whitman in jail over night. His last statement was enough for her to claim suspicion; the threat to kill two people. She wanted to talk to him in the morning, when she was more alert and he was more scared, see what she could get out of him. If he didn't lawyer up. She was sure he didn't have his own lawyer, but he could still ask for one. If he did, she'd be looking long and hard at him for the murder of Tammy Lee.

She also needed to talk to Andrew again. She kept getting conflicting reports about his relationship with Tammy Lee. He said he broke up with the girl while in Afghanistan. According to Amy, her sister Bria said she thought Tammy Lee broke up with Andrew, but then said her sister still talked about him all the time. The parents said she broke up with him, as did Terry.

But then why was the ring in his car? Had it slipped off her finger when he drove her home, or had she purposefully taken it off and dropped it so she'd have a reason to see him again, to let him know she was available?

Andrew hadn't seemed proud of the fact that he had broken off their relationship—and of course, she was inclined to believe him—but who would tell her the truth? Maybe she should talk to Tammy Lee's sister herself?

Claire took some bread out of the wrapper and put a couple of pieces in the toaster, then she got out the peanut butter and cherry jelly. She needed to eat something. She thought about having a glass of wine, but somehow it didn't seem to go with her sandwich, so she settled instead for milk.

She sat at the counter eating her peanut butter and jelly sandwich and thought about the Burning Boat. Somehow it made her so sad that she had been enjoying the flames peaking into the sky, not knowing that a body was being burned as hundreds of people stood and watched. She wondered if they would ever dare do another Burning Boat celebration.

When she was finished with her toast and had licked her fingers, then washed her hands, she got out her notes on the case. Bria Johansen, a Minnesota number. What had Amy told her—the woman lived in Hastings and was a school teacher. Sounded reliable.

A woman answered on the second ring. Claire told her who she was and why she calling.

"Do you know anything more?" Bria said. "I'm having a very hard time believing this has happened to Tammy Lee."

"We're working very hard to find out who would do this to your sister. I'm so sorry."

"Thank you. Tammy Lee and I weren't very close, but I know I'll miss her all my life. You just do."

"Yes, you just do." Claire resisted thinking about her first husband who had been killed.

"Do you get used to it, being a cop?" Bria asked.

"Not really. I'm often surprised by how much I come to feel like I know the person who has died, even though I've never met them."

"Tammy Lee was a pistol."

"So I've heard. What about Terry, her fiancé? How did you get along with him?"

"Oh, we didn't have much in common, but he seemed okay. He was on the same wavelength with Tammy Lee and could keep up with her."

"What about Andrew? Andrew Stickler? Did you know him?"

"Oh, of course I knew Andrew. He was a sweetheart. I think I was nearly as sad as Tammy Lee was when they broke up."

"So who called it quits, and why?"

"Well, Tammy Lee claimed she was the one who sent a text to him, but I've always had my doubts. She seemed pretty crazy about him. To tell you the truth, I'm not sure they would have stayed together much longer if he had not gone off to war. You don't think Andrew had anything to do with this, do you?"

"We're just checking out everyone. Had they been in touch much since he'd been back?"

"I guess a little. I think he gave her a ride home one night. She said something about getting together with him at the Burning Boat. I wasn't surprised. I don't think there were any hard feelings between them."

"We found her engagement ring in his car."

Bria made a sharp intake of breath. "That's where it went. Tammy Lee said she dropped it. I wonder if she did it on purpose. To tell you the truth, I think she still had a thing for Andrew."

"Do you think Terry knew this?"

"Tammy didn't tend to keep quiet about her feelings. He might have."

"Do you know if Terry was ever violent with Tammy Lee?"

Bria stayed quiet for a few moments. "I've been thinking about that ever since I heard how Tammy Lee died. I don't know if he ever hit her, but he could be terribly jealous. She called here crying one night, this was about a half a year ago, saying she was going to leave him. I guess she had been talking to another guy at the bar when he got off work, and he went ballistic. I told her she could come and stay with me. Next thing I knew, everything was fine. Wasn't long after that he bought her the ring. She was anxious to get married. Then Andrew came back and she seemed to be having second thoughts."

"Is there anyone else we should be looking at?"

"I can't think why anyone would want to kill her. She really just wanted to have fun, like that song."

છ

Meg ordered a burger and the three of them went to sit in a booth. Andrew squeezed in next to Meg, and Doug sat across from them. Meg was surprised that Andrew and Doug were friends.

They just seemed and looked so different. Andrew was calm and smooth where Doug was like choppy water.

"So you already got another girlfriend?" Doug said, tapping his fingers on the table like he was playing a piano.

Meg thought this was rather an odd question and was curious how Andrew would answer it. She wondered if she was his new girlfriend.

Andrew put down his hamburger and said, "What'd you mean, another?"

"I remember that Tammy Lee. How hot she was. You talked about her. You showed me her picture."

"Remember, I broke up with her."

"Yeah, but she kept writing you. I thought for sure you'd get back together when you got back home."

"No chance of that now. She's dead."

Doug's forehead wrinkled. His hand stopped tapping as he lifted it to his face and wiped his eyes. "Really? I saw her just a while ago. Tracked her down. When you threw her picture out, I kept it."

"When did you see her?" Meg couldn't help asking. She had noticed that Doug hadn't asked how she had died.

Doug turned her way, but his eyes were darting around the room. Meg felt his nervous energy like a buzzing electrical current. "I don't know. The days run together. Like not quite a week ago."

Meg knew the day Tammy Lee had died; she couldn't help keeping track of her mother's work. "Friday?"

"Could be."

"Did you talk to her when you tracked her down?" Andrew asked.

"Sure. We talked about you. I told her about the vow and how you had broke it. I wanted her to understand that you weren't good enough for her."

Andrew leaned forward and Meg was glad there was a table between the two men. He looked like he wanted to hurt Doug. "Doug, why?"

"I'm not going to forget it, Andrew. I saw what you did. I watched it happen. You let Brian die."

Andrew pushed himself out of the booth and stood, looking down at Doug. "What did you see? What do you think you saw?"

Doug stood up, too, and they were face to face. Andrew was clenching his fists and Meg was afraid he was going to punch Doug. "We promised each other that we would do everything we could to get through the war together. We made a vow that we would go together. You promised, and you broke it."

"I kept my vow."

"No, you didn't," Doug screamed. "You let go of Brian. You could have saved him, but you let him fall and then they shot him. They shot him over and over again, and you let it happen. He's dead because of you. I know. I was there."

"Doug, that isn't what happened." Andrew held himself back as he spoke slowly.

Then Doug pulled out the gun.

ᘐ

When Rich stood up from the bar to leave, he saw that Meg, Andrew, and the scrawny guy had settled in a booth. Should he stop by and say something to them? Would he tell Claire about this when he got home? He hated to be in the middle between mother and daughter, and it didn't happen very often.

As he stood there watching them talk, it looked like the conversation was getting a little heated. Then Andrew lunged out of the booth, and a moment later the other guy did, too. They were facing each other, almost touching, air crackling around them. Meg was starting to get out of the booth.

Rich was getting a very bad feeling. The scrawny guy sucked in air around him like a black hole. He was headed toward something that had nothing to do with what was happening in the bar.

Then the guy pulled out a gun.

Rich reached in his coat for his cell phone and with just a glance punched in the code for Claire's number.

Time to call in the posse.

CHAPTER 22

Claire registered Rich saying three words—"Meg, Fort, gun"—
and she was out the door without her coat, her car keys in one
hand, her gun in the other.

She ran to the squad car and then stood for one full long second
outside the door, tilted her head up, and prayed to whatever was
up there that could help her. Then she was in the car and careening
backward down the driveway. As she turned the car toward Fort
St. Antoine, she put in a call for backup. Heaven help anyone on
the road with her.

It took her just over a minute to get the Fort, but she noticed
everything, the cars swaying by going the other direction, the
blur of the trees on the sides of the road, the road like a corridor
she was headed down, the dotted line in the middle of the road
beating a pulse in her head.

She forced herself to slow down as she raced into town and
pulled up behind a pickup truck right outside the Fort. Again, a
breath. She needed to be calm to save her daughter. Her darling
daughter. Meg. Nothing could go wrong. She couldn't live if it
did.

Peeking in the window she saw Andrew and another guy talking
with Meg standing in between them. Why did her daughter have
to be there? She had warned her about Andrew. Claire couldn't see

the gun, but assumed it was hidden from her view. She had to act as if it was pointed at someone and take every precaution.

Claire ran to the back of the Fort and went in through the kitchen. A lanky teenaged cook was pulling something out of the deep fryer. She clamped her hand over his mouth, then whispered to him, "Get out of here right now. Go out front and when the other deputies come, have them wait for me to signal them."

She shoved him toward the back door and hoped he had the sense not to let the door slam. Claire ducked down, slipped through the doorway into the main room, and snuck up behind the bar.

When she peeked over the wooden countertop, she saw that a blond guy who looked more than half crazed had the gun pointed at Meg, and Andrew was trying to talk him down. Meg had frozen. It was worse than Claire had imagined, and she had to push all such thoughts away.

Claire pulled out her gun and got ready.

જી

Meg couldn't believe this guy was pointing a gun at her. She almost wanted to laugh, just to break the horrible tension in the air, to not believe it was real. But she could tell from Andrew's reaction to him that this Doug was a live wire and apt to go off at any second.

She was hearing what they were saying, but she wasn't really comprehending it. Words washed through her like glass beads of fear. She was still alive. They were still talking. She was still breathing. Focus on that.

It sounded like Doug was still fighting in the war. That's all she could figure. He hadn't been able to come home. He blamed Andrew for something horrible. A friend of theirs had been killed, and Doug thought it was Andrew's fault. And then all this talk of a vow, that they would all go down together. Just like Andrew had explained in the barn.

Doug was pointing the gun at her, but he was looking at Andrew. He said he would kill her, because that way Andrew would hurt the worst. Just like he had killed his other girlfriend.

Meg raised her hand as if she could stop him from doing something. Then she pointed at the hole at the end of the gun barrel. Maybe it was like in the cartoons where if you put your finger in the end, the gun exploded.

She didn't know what else to do. She couldn't say any words.

So she reached out and put her finger on the end of the gun.

෴

Andrew remembered that last firefight in Afghanistan in flashes. They had walked into an ambush. Doug was shot immediately. Then Brian started to go over the edge of a cliff and Andrew tried to grab him, flinging out his hand. Brian's hand grabbed his, and he hung over the drop. Andrew was lying flat on the ground, and Brian's fingers were squeezing his wrist. The drag on his arm was tearing something deep inside of him. The barrage of bullets thickened in the air. With every breath, Andrew commanded his hand to hold on, and then he felt a slip.

Brian's fingers flew free.

He let go of Andrew's hand.

And without his help, Andrew couldn't hold him.

Brian dropped.

As his body fell away, it was pelted by bullets that tore him into pieces. Andrew watched until it hit the rocks and tumbled like a bag of hay, tearing apart.

Brian had left them.

He had to convince Doug of what happened. He had to keep talking, keep Doug listening to him, looking at him. "I didn't let go of Brian. Don't you get it? Brian did. He let go of me."

Doug heard him and said, "He let go of you?"

"Yes. I was holding on to him tight and he had hold of my wrist, but then he let go. I couldn't hold him after that. He slipped out of my hand."

"He did it?"

Andrew nodded. "I think he did it for me. So I wouldn't get hurt."

Doug looked down at the gun he was holding.

Then Meg reached out and put her finger over the end of the barrel.

℧

Claire only heard silence. She tried to think of how to handle this situation, but it was like her mind was scattered points of energy. This was not a time for thinking, this was a time for doing.

Claire stood up and shouted, "Stop."

When nothing changed, when only Meg turned and looked at her, Claire moved to step two.

She lifted her gun over the edge of the bar.

Now, they all looked at her: Meg, Andrew and the guy with the gun.

Meg moved as Claire pulled on the trigger.

The noise of her gun filled the whole room—twice as loud as it should have been.

CHAPTER 23

Rich saw it all happen. He had resisted stepping in until Meg was in the middle of it. He started across the room, and then he watched as Meg put her finger on the barrel of the gun. That stopped him. She had put herself in harm's way. Any movement from him could make it worse.

Then Claire stood up behind the bar and shouted some loud word. It only registered as noise. Meg turned, saw her mother. The two men looked at Claire, and in that instant so many things happened:

Claire raised her gun, Meg stepped forward and pushed down on the barrel of the gun, the guy with the gun fell back, and two guns went off.

Like a frozen tableau, they all stayed where they were except for the guy. He landed on the floor in a heap. The silence was broken by his sobs. His gun was still in his hands.

Rich wasn't sure, but it looked like no one had gotten hurt. He could see no blood.

Andrew moved first. He reached down and took the gun away from his buddy. Then he put an arm around his shoulders.

Meg ran to her mother, and Claire climbed over the bar to get to her. They held onto each other and rocked. Rich walked over and put his arms around both of them, holding them as tight as he could.

When they broke apart, Claire put her hands on Meg's face and said, "You're okay?"

"I pushed the gun down. I think it shot a hole in the floor."

"Oh, Meggy, I was so scared."

"So was I, Mom, but I wasn't going to let him shoot me."

Rich wrapped an arm around her neck. "You're as tough as your mom. You're always going to be okay."

✧

Andrew squatted on the floor, holding on to Doug.

Claire walked over, took the gun from Andrew and asked him, "Who is this guy?"

"Doug Nelson. A guy I knew in Afghanistan. I think he killed Tammy Lee. Because of me."

"He tell you that?"

"Kind of."

"What happened to him?"

How did he begin to explain what happened to Doug? "I'm not sure. We were in a bad ambush together, and he was wounded. They flew him out and I haven't seen him until now."

"How did he know Tammy Lee?"

"Because I talked about her, and because of a picture I showed him when we were over there."

"Why did he kill her, then?"

"Because he wanted to hurt me."

"How would that hurt you?"

"Tammy made the big mistake of telling him that she and I were getting back together again."

"Was this true?"

"Not at all. But I'm so sorry." And then something sprung open in him, a well, a river of tears started pouring down his face.

He bent his head over Doug's shoulders and said, "I'm so sorry, buddy. I'm so sorry."

☙

Amy pushed past the teenaged boy in an apron who was trying to tell her to wait, to not go in until she was told to. She had heard shots and she was going in.

When she slammed open the door, she was surprised at the scene she saw. Rich was holding Meg in his arms, and she was tucked into his chest like a bird.

Claire was standing over two men, who were folded over each other and crying. One of them was Andrew. She didn't recognize the other guy.

"Do I need to call an ambulance?" she asked Claire.

Claire just shook her head.

"What happened?"

Claire looked at Amy and didn't know where to start. "It's a long story, going way back to the war. All the wounds they brought home."

CHAPTER 24

"I didn't mean to kill her, just to knock some sense into her," Doug said as Claire drove him back to the sheriff's department.

She had tried to keep him from talking, wanting to get back to the department and on the record, but finally decided it didn't matter. She had read him his rights, and there seemed no stopping him. He had to keep going over and over what he had done, like he was throwing it up.

"She wouldn't give up on Andrew. I told her what he had done, how he had broken the vow, but she just laughed at me. Said I was crazy. I knew I was, but I knew what I knew. That Andrew had to pay for what he had done."

"So what happened?"

"I was going to leave. I was at her house, but I was walking out the door and I tried one more time to persuade her. She was pushing me out the door, so I pushed back. I guess I pushed pretty hard because she fell straight backwards and cracked her head. I heard it hit the floor. I tried to get her to move, but she wouldn't, so I left."

"Are you sure she was dead?"

There was silence from the back seat. Claire glanced up into the rearview mirror and could see Doug nodding. Finally he said, "I know what dead people look like. I know what they feel like. Empty. She was dead."

"Did you take her body with you?"

"No way. Why would I do that? Nobody knows me here. 'Cept Andrew. And I didn't really care anyway. That's why I'm telling you. See, I should have died over there. That's what the vow was all about. We either all make it, or none of us do. I should have died when Brian did, but Andrew dragged me out. Then I don't remember nothing. Next time I come to I'm in Germany, for God's sake."

"You didn't go back to Tammy Lee's house and take her to the Burning Boat?" Claire asked him again.

"I don't know what you're talking about. I didn't take her any place. I left her on the floor. Figured someone would find her soon enough. I hoped it would be Andrew. Then he would see what he had done. Then he would know."

He fell silent and Claire watched a car come at her, dim its lights, then drive past. The countryside was dark with no moon, no stars, just black. She didn't want to talk to this crazy guy anymore. Something wasn't fitting together. But why would he claim to have killed Tammy Lee if he hadn't? And if he did, then who put her body in the Burning Boat?

"Andrew should pay," Doug mumbled.

"What?" Claire asked, not sure she was quite hearing him.

"It's all Andrew's fault. I don't have a life anymore. And he shouldn't have one, either."

Claire didn't want to argue with Doug. She tried not to think of a time and a place that could create such thoughts in a man. A war that stole lives and then just kept taking them, even after it was over, even after the soldiers were safely home.

∽

"Was I wrong?" Andrew asked Meg. After Claire had taken Doug away, they had returned to their seats in the booth. Andrew looked at the hole in the floor and the one in the wall and still couldn't quite believe what had just happened.

"Wrong about what?" Meg asked.

He could see she was shivering. He stood up and gave her his jean jacket. She wrapped it around her shoulders and looked at him with her big eyes.

"So many things," Andrew started, the list seeming to grow endless in his mind. "Going to war. Making that stupid vow. Watching Brian die. Not taking better care of Doug. And then meeting him here, in public. Bringing you into it."

"I don't know about all those things. You'll just have to figure them out. But I don't think you could've taken care of Doug, and I'm glad you didn't meet him by yourself." She ducked her head and said, "Then you might be dead." She started to cry.

Rich Haggard walked over and put a hand on Meg's shoulder. "I think it's time I took her home."

Andrew knew he couldn't argue with Rich. As much as he wanted to take her in his arms and hold her so tight, he knew he had no right. Maybe he never had. "Yeah, I think she's in shock."

"I think we all are," Rich said, not unkindly.

"I'll talk to you tomorrow," Andrew said.

Meg wiped at her face, but just smeared the tears around. Her mouth quivered, but she nodded.

"I'm sorry," Andrew said, hoping it would begin to help. "I'm so sorry this happened to you."

Meg shook her head. "You need to take care of yourself right now. I know you're sorry, but don't worry about me."

She stood up and gave him back his jacket. Rich wrapped an arm around her shoulder, and they walked together out the front door.

Andrew sat still and felt like waves of sand and blood were washing over him. How would he ever dig out of this life?

∞

Claire got up early the next morning. Neither Meg nor Rich were awake when she left for work. She wanted this case to be over, and she wanted the truth. She wanted to know what exactly had happened to Tammy Lee.

She had one of the guards get Terry Whitman up as soon as she got to the department. "Put him in the interrogation room. Don't let him pee. Don't give him anything to eat or drink. Let him sit there for a while."

After an hour she decided she couldn't wait any longer. She opened the door and Terry jumped at the sight of her.

Claire sat across the table from Terry and turned the recorder on. She sat quietly, letting it sink into Terry where he was and why. He looked like he hadn't slept much last night. That was good. The defenses would be falling away. A little quiet would allow more of them to drop off.

Finally she said, "I don't think you killed Tammy Lee."

He looked up at her with a glimmer of hope in his eyes. She was hooking him with it, reeling him in.

"I didn't kill her. I swear I didn't."

"What happened then, Terry? Explain it to me. When did you meet up with Tammy Lee on Thursday night?"

"I got off work. We met like usual at the bar. She'd liked to get out and I wasn't good for much, but I wanted to have a drink or two. But right away we start arguing. She reminds me she lost the ring. Do you know how much I paid for that ring? I couldn't believe it. I couldn't tell if she was playing with me. She liked to do that."

"I bet you were pretty mad about the ring."

"I was. I asked her where she thought she lost it. She wouldn't say at first, but then she mentions Andrew, how he gave her a ride home. She says maybe she lost it in his car. She's been teasing me about Andrew ever since he got back, saying how good he was at everything. Anyway, we go back to her house. All I want to do is go to sleep, but she wants to goof around. She starts telling me how good Andrew was in bed. She makes it sound like they did something recently. I just lost it. The ring and Andrew, and now this. I knew if I stuck around we'd just get into a fight. So I left."

"Was that the last time you saw her?"

Terry looked lost. He stared around the room as if he could find something to hold on to. "Not exactly."

"You didn't hurt her before you left, did you?"

"Not really. She was coming at me when I got to the door so I just pushed her away, and then I slammed the door. I was surprised when she didn't come after me, but I just wanted to get home and go to sleep. I didn't push her that hard. I don't know what happened to her."

"Did you go back to Tammy Lee's house?"

He shook his head, but not as a negative gesture, more to shake the thoughts away.

"Terry, did you see Tammy after that?"

"When I woke up the next morning, I called, but she didn't answer the phone. I let it ring until the answering machine picked up. But that got me worried. I was sure she was there and just didn't want to talk to me. So I went over to her place."

"What did you find?"

"I don't know. I just don't know how it happened. I didn't push her that hard. Just like a get-away shove, not even mean or anything." His eyes were staring at something that wasn't in the room. He sucked in his breath and then said, "I opened the door and there she was, lying on the floor."

He pulled his eyes away from this image and looked up at Claire. "She was dead, but I swear I didn't do it. But how else could it have happened?"

"What did you do?"

"I was scared. I knew everyone would think I did it. We were at the bar together. I would get blamed. I had to get rid of the body. So I came up with this idea about the Burning Boat."

"How did you know about it?"

"Oh, everybody talks about it, plus I had brought over some lumber from the rail yard. I thought if I could get her body in to the boat, it would disappear in the fire. It would all go away. Tammy would be gone, but she has done that before, just run off. People might think I did it, but there would be no body."

"But there are bones, and we know they're Tammy's."

His shoulders sank, his head slumped, he sighed. "I can't believe I killed her."

"I don't think you did."

He lifted his head up. "Why? Did that Andrew have something to do with it?"

"No, but a friend of his did. Or rather, someone who was in the service with him." Then Claire explained what Doug had done.

"So he must have come right after I left," Terry said.

Claire said, "Must have."

"If I would have stayed, she'd still be alive."

"Maybe, or maybe you'd both be dead."

CHAPTER 25

His desk was the same desk he had been given when he joined the sheriff's department thirty years ago, and it had been battered and old then. The top drawer never slid in easily, you always had to jiggle it. He still banged his knee on the pencil drawer when he sat down. He had probably touched the desk more than he had caressed his wife, even cried more on its gray frame.

Talbert could just see himself taking the desk home. His wife had told him he could have Kent's old room to do what he wanted with, and she would say nothing if he brought home the desk, just point him to the basement and clench her mouth tight.

She would try to give him space, but the house was her domain. Maybe Kent's room would work out. He could set up a workroom in the basement, maybe do some woodworking like he had always wanted to.

He wasn't sure what the doctors had told his wife, but she was adamant that he retire. "It's time for us to be together," she had said.

"And do what?" he asked.

She looked thoughtful for a moment, then said, "Jigsaw puzzles. We both like them."

As Talbert sat at his old desk, a day filled with puzzles and carved bowls sounded like he'd be spending a lot of time in front of the TV and napping. He didn't want to go to sleep for the rest of his life.

But he knew he had to give up the job. He had given it up. It was time for him to move on, and let Claire Watkins take over as sheriff. She was ready, and she still had the energy, and, as far as he knew, her heart was beating strong.

He looked up and she was standing in the doorway. "May I come in?" she asked.

"Hey, it's your office."

"Doesn't feel like it."

"Make it your own," he suggested. "Maybe get a new desk."

She walked in and ran a hand down the surface of the desk. "I might do that. Have Rich make me a desk."

"Then you won't mind if I take this one. Get it out of your way?"

"That would be great. I guess I'll have to make some changes, and we might as well start with the desk."

He stood up. "I'll come and get it in a day or two."

"I might need you to come in a few times a week to help me settle in," Claire said.

"Be glad to do that."

"I'm not sure . . . ."

He put his hand on her shoulder and wasn't sure he had ever touched her before, other than to shake her hand. "You're going to be great. You were made for this job. Just took a heart attack for me to see that. Plus, I have been making plans for my retirement."

Her face brightened. "Oh, yes, that sounds good. Are you going to travel?"

"Might. The wife doesn't like airplanes much, but we could take the train."

"What else?"

He scrambled. He didn't want to sound like a loser, playing jigsaw puzzles. "I've been thinking of learning Latin."

"Wow," Claire said.

"Yeah, I've never learned another language and that is supposed to be the mother of them all."

"Maybe you'll become a scholar."

He laughed. "From sheriff to scholar. Could happen."

"Just let me know if you need any help with clearing up in here," she said as she backed out the door.

"Good job on the Whitman case."

"Thanks."

"You do good work, Claire."

❧

Meg watched Andrew as he walked through the crowd of people at the Fort. He was such a good man. He listened to people. He believed in things. He had even fought for them.

He stopped and talked to Mrs. Baumgarden. The old woman put her small hand on his arm and he patted it. He didn't try to rush away. Even though he knew Meg was there, across the room, waiting for him.

Meg had known what she had to do, but now she knew it more deeply. She couldn't be with Andrew. She wasn't ready. Everybody made a big deal that he was eight years older than her, but the years didn't matter. What was insurmountable was that he had been to a country that she hoped never to visit—a land of danger and dying. Desolate in a way that no place should be.

She was not ready to take on such a man, such a place, such despair.

Andrew hugged Mrs. Baumgarden, said goodbye, and then strode quickly to Meg's side.

"Hey, you made it," he said. "Can you stay?"

"Just for a moment."

With those words, he knew. She could tell by the way he turned his head to look at the crowd. "Busy here tonight," he said.

"Yeah, everybody heard what happened here. I guess they want to see the holes for themselves."

"Wouldn't surprise me if they just leave the holes for souvenirs," Andrew said, laughing.

"Andrew," Meg started.

He put a finger on her lips. "You don't have to say anything. I'm so sorry you had to witness what you did, but so glad to have known you. You're off on a big adventure, and I am too. I'm starting therapy at the VA and I'll probably be living in the Twin Cities while I do that. I thought I could jump right back into real life, but I guess I have to deal with what happened over there."

"You're going to do great," Meg said, wishing she could say more.

"So are you," he said.

He leaned down and kissed her on the top of her head, and she knew it would have to do for now. They were going very separate ways, but what they had shared together they would keep.

༄

Claire stood and watched him digging on the shoreline. It was past ten o'clock and one of the campers had called her at home to report a man doing something strange on the beach.

"I called the mayor first, but he told me to call you," the woman told her.

"Yes, I can take care of it," Claire said, as she was pretty sure she knew who it was and what he was doing.

She would let him finish his task before she stepped in to stop him. She guessed why he was doing it, and she agreed with him. There was a reason that ashes were so often scattered over water. Yes, we came from and went back to dust. But in the beginning, we come out of the water.

Claire could tell it was Terry Whitman from the shape of his body, slightly bent over, and that cap he was wearing on his head. The lime green color of it showed up fluorescent under the dim overhead lights of the campground.

He had been charged with accessory after the fact, but the judge had let him go on his own reconnaissance. Because he had a home and a job, he wasn't seen as much of a flight risk.

Possibly what he was doing right now was illegal, but Claire wasn't going to turn him in for it. We all mourn in our own ways, we all try to take care of what little was left to do when the person we love dies. She figured throwing some dirt in Lake Pepin was a pretty innocent way to acknowledge all he had lost.

After a few more shovelfuls, he stopped to leaned on the handle and stare out across the lake. The night was quiet and the lake was calm. Clear enough to see the opposite shore. She breathed deeply and took in the cool autumn air. The weatherman said it might go below freezing tonight, and she believed it. No clouds in the sky to hold in the warmth.

Slowly she walked up to him, making some noise so she wouldn't startle him. "Hey, Terry."

He turned, dropped the shovel, and said, "I just had to take care of this."

"Fine. But now it's time to stop and go home."

"Tammy would have liked to go up in flames. I mean, not at her age, not so young, but she would have liked the drama of it. She always said she wanted to be cremated, and she was really into the natural stuff."

"That's nice," Claire said. "A good way to look at it."

"I'm not sorry for what I did, even if I did it for the wrong reasons and even if I have to pay for it. Going up in ashes with the Burning Boat would have pleased her."

Claire waited.

"And she loved the lake. She wanted to get married down here by the lake. I thought it was a goofy idea, why not just a church like regular people, but she insisted we do it by the lake."

"Sounds like it would have been nice."

"You know, I loved her. And she did love me. In her own way. Andrew was just her past, and she would have gotten over him."

"Hmm," Claire agreed.

"We would have been happy." He put the shovel over his shoulder and headed to his car.

CHAPTER 26

"Do you know how many people I killed over there?" Doug asked.

Claire was standing back, behind Doug so he wouldn't be too aware of her there. She was glad to see that Doug was talking. He hadn't said much to her this morning. She was afraid he was going to clam up with the psychiatrist she had brought in to evaluate him.

"No," Dr. Fallow said, then waited. Fallow was a young woman who wore her hair pulled back tight and a blue blazer like a Catholic schoolgirl, but she was very sharp and persistent. She also knew when to shut up and listen.

"I don't either. I lost count. I couldn't keep remembering. Sometimes I didn't know if I killed them. Maybe they didn't die."

"I'm sorry."

"I did it for my country. I guess. Mainly I just did it so I'd stay alive."

"So why did you kill your grandmother?" Dr. Fallow asked, quietly.

"I've already told the cops."

"I need to hear it, too. From you. To see if you are sane, as I've told you. In your own words."

"I don't mind. Simple. She didn't want to live anymore. I couldn't take care of her any other way. Her life was over, but her body hadn't quit yet. That's all. I know she wanted me to end it, but she just didn't know how to ask."

"How did you know?"

"Because I loved her and I could tell she had had enough. I could tell because I've had enough." He crumpled in his chair. "I don't want to live anymore, either. I wish I would have died over there. Then I'd be a hero. Now I'm just a criminal. What's the difference? Where you kill someone? Whether you kill them because you love them or you hate them? What if you kill them and you don't even know them? What makes that right?"

"I don't have the answers to those questions." Fallows looked down and spread a hand out on the table. "Did you know what you were doing when you shot her?"

"Sure I did. I waited until she was sleeping and then I took my grandfather's gun and shot her."

"What about Tammy Lee Johansen?"

"Well, that was different."

"How so?"

"It was an accident. I didn't really know her, just from a picture. I didn't really mean to kill her, just to scare her away from Andrew."

"Who's Andrew?"

"One of my best buddies. He and I and Brian vowed we'd get through the war together, or go down fighting."

"Sounds like you all went down fighting."

"I guess. I don't know anymore. I thought Andrew had let go of Brian, but he says that Brian let him go. Maybe Brian changed his mind. Maybe he just wanted to die, too." Doug shook his head. "I'm sorry that girl died. I'm sorry that Brian died. I hope Andrew does okay. He was always a good guy. Even when I hated him, I still liked him."

❦

The sheriff's office was hers now. Pretty spare. Claire had moved her desk off the floor and brought it into the office. Maybe someday Rich would have time to make her a nicer desk, but right now she had work to do.

She had brought an old wingback chair from home and put it in the corner of the room, with an afghan her mother had crocheted spread on it. With a lamp behind it, it would make a nice place to read and to have people wait for her. She knew it was a feminine touch, but decided there was nothing wrong with that.

A designer she had been friends with believed that a more homey environment created an atmosphere of civility. Lord knows, we need more civility, she thought.

Two straight-backed chairs sat opposite her desk. Not too comfortable, but solid.

Two pictures sat on the top of the bookshelf: Rich, sitting amongst a flock of pheasants, smiling his generous smile, and Meg, lounging on the deck with flowers that she had picked in her hair. She was sixteen in the photo, and even though Claire knew she could not keep her daughter that age, she was so glad to have the picture of her happy daughter.

The door was left open, a new custom she had started. She only closed the door when she was in a private conversation, or when she was gone. She had gotten used to the hum of noise on the floor and liked to hear it in the background. Plus she wanted to be accessible, available to her deputies.

A knock came on the frame of the door, and then Andrew Stickler poked his head around the corner.

"Hey," he said.

"Come on in. I'm just getting settled."

"Congratulations," he said, still standing.

"Have a seat," she offered.

"I can't stay long. Just came in to say goodbye and thanks for all your help. I'm moving up to the Cities. I've got a part-time job as a night security guard. I appreciated the letter of recommendation."

"No problem."

"I'm also starting therapy at the VA."

"I hope that goes well." After thinking for a moment, she decided she would tell him he was not alone. "Quite a few years ago I was in therapy for nearly a year. It helped. I sorted some things out. But it's hard work."

"Nothing could be harder than what I've been through."

She smiled. "Except going through it again. But with someone else at your side."

"Yeah. Is Meg gone?"

"She leaves tonight."

"Give her my best."

"I will."

"I'm sorry I kept seeing her."

"I know it wasn't just you. Meg has talked to me about it."

"Oh, I guess she would. You have a lovely daughter."

"I know."

"Is Doug going to be okay?"

"Hard to say. He's been evaluated and found to have severe PTSD. I'm not sure how that's going to affect the judge's decision at his hearing."

"He was a good soldier."

"I know." If she hadn't been standing behind the desk, Claire would have reached out and hugged him. But she was the sheriff now, and the desk was there between them. "I wish you well, Andrew. Let us know how you're doing."

She reached across the desk and they shook hands.
"I will." He turned and walked out of the room.

&

Claire was just going to embrace Meg one last time at the door,
kiss her on the forehead, wish her well, and let her go. Which she
did. But then as the car backed out of the driveway, she couldn't
stop herself, she couldn't stay in the house while Meg drove out of
her life, off to college for the first time.

So just as the car turned onto the highway, disappearing from
sight, Claire bolted out the door. She ran down the driveway and
caught sight of the shadow of the car, aimed south on Highway
35, carrying her sweet daughter off into the night.

She watched the taillights of the car, twin stars, until the bend
in the road took them away.